DOG DAYS IN CUBA

A Quest for Treasure

Paulina A. Zelitsky

ISNB: 978-1-7770356-9-3

Dedication:

To all my long-suffering sisters and brothers in Cuba.

Table of Contents

Prologue

It may surprise you to learn that this story is being recounted to you by a chocolate brown male Doberman - Benz, as in Mercedez-Benz. My human pack calls me just Benz because, they said, "the name 'Mercedez-Benz is already patented." How I got to be named in honor of an iconic car company is a good story, which I will get to shortly. Meanwhile, I want to make it clear the real reason my human pack has chosen me to share with you my working-dog adventures in Cuba is their hope my canine language might suffer lesser censorship. So, you will have to forgive me for some of my canine languages, which you might find difficult to translate.

Dora, my adoptive Mommy, rescued me from a horrible fate. The Caribbean Island, where I was born, should have been 'a paradise island', but in reality, the paradise in Cuba is only for '*yumas*' (the foreign tourists); for the majority of ordinary Cubans, it is '*a Caribbean Gulag*'. Dora remedied my status by legally adopting me, and this elevated me into the privileged foreign caste, but the truth is I was born just east of Havana in a village of Cojimar - where Ernest Hemingway kept his famous fishing boat, El Pilar. The chance association was to become a useful addition to my literary resume.

My original native owners were determined to dock my tail off and have my ears clipped. This proposed mutilation was meant to be a canine fashion statement, which later struck me as incongruous in the context of what looked like a George Booth cartoon from The New Yorker - a poor, small dusty village of stray cats and dogs and ramshackle houses. At the time, I was only a few weeks old and ignorant of the social significance of designer dogs. Anyway, Providence came to my assistance when a foreign lady offered to buy me from my Cuban owner. For sixty-five American dollars, I was spared surgical trauma and spirited off to a massive art deco house on a hill overlooking the beach in the gated community of Tarara in Habana del Este.

Mommy's overwhelming kindness did not prepare me for the domestic firestorm that occasioned my arrival in my new home. Mommy Dora is married to Daddy Frank - a nice-looking, middle-aged Jewish man who fancies himself a social philosopher. You may imagine my embarrassment when I heard angry shouts: "You bring that Nazi dog into this house, and I am leaving. It's me or this dog."

Had I been a few months older, I would have expected at least a shred of Talmudic compassion from this irate man. As it was, only confusion descended on my still-tender soul. Within a week or two, however, anger became irritation, then quiet acceptance, then kindness, and finally love, when I moved into his queen-sized bed for my nightly sojourn with Daddy. Alas, with the human race, so much canine patience is required.

Most of the Cuban employees of our foreign Joint Venture in Cuba, I am proud to note, welcomed me immediately with smiles and open arms. Notwithstanding the loving disposition of my new human family, everyone was totally surprised when their stunning discoveries were made possible with the new advanced deep ocean survey technology combined with my exceptional extrasensory canine ability beyond the realm of current mechanical physics.

I will do my very best to describe these events to you; still, I want to ask the reader who will find my stories incredulous and my technical descriptions boring not to blame for it the rest of my poor dog kind considering the impact of my very close association with my human scientific family, always interested in dangerous attractions of discovering the new. It is also very important to point out that my scientific endeavors were given on a purely voluntary basis, for I love to learn, explore, and want to please my human pack to the best of my abilities.

Wearing my Brain Clone Helmet, containing the Brain-Computer Interface (developed especially for me by my dear friends - young Cuban programmers, scientists, and engineers), permitted me to discriminate minor neural electrical signals in my brain decode this information, and send it to a computer. This is how the Brain Clone Helmet enabled our communication and commenced my writing carrier. Reactions of my human pack – my teammates, were not always positive and supportive. They started hiding their important, personal discussions from me because they were afraid, I will publish their opinions on the internet.

It is not that I ever intended to publish anything critical about them; quite the opposite, I respect, share, and obey them most of the time. My comments have no ill intent, but, unfortunately, my humble canine expressions and lack of human diplomacy could have been misinterpreted as aggressive or conflictive. My teammates' reason is, "if the Cuban authorities think that our dog repeats what he sees and hears from his human companions, they will punish all of us." Sorry, humans in this country are always scared and not of me! On this notice, permit me to thank my human pack for many hours of training, protecting me, and for their dedication to developing my scientific interest and intellect.

Chapter 1

April 1997, Havana

Today in our home, we received a very important Cuban boss - Comandante Tainted, and his lovely family for the Sunday meal. Cubans secretly call him Tainted to reflect on his losing status of Top Dog when he returned to Cuba from abroad, where, as I understand, he sinned by rolling in some western poop.

I was asked to display my best possible behavior and wear my new golden-colored bowtie, made by our housekeeper Vera, especially for this occasion. Motherly-natured Vera - our housekeeper, is a blond, slim, petite, sweet, but very practical Cuban woman. She smells wonderful from cooking food and is very feminine, wearing a long cotton dress, apron, and headscarf. Before her employment with us, she worked as a Professor of Economics at Cuban College. Her profession made her particularly conscient about values and sensitivities in the Cuban revolutionary style. She pretends that I am one of her students and constantly lectures me on the national economy, rules of proper behavior, hygiene, and etiquette. She makes me dizzy with her promises of rewards in the future while I am more interested in real-time rewards, such as food. To be honest, I am a Cuban and learned to take all virtual promises with a pinch of salt in my mouth.

Still, I shall admit being very fond of the house my adoptive parents are leasing in Tarara – a Cuban health tourist resort for foreigners near Havana. According to the commentaries I overheard, the original owner of our house was Carlos Prío Socarrás, the first and the last democratic ex-president of Cuba. His two-story, four-bedroom house on the top of a hill is spacious and light with a wide marble staircase leading to a marble floor hall – perfect for my sliding across. A large marble terrace around the house perimeter rises above the resort facilities and offers an unobstructed view of the Atlantic Ocean. Roberto, my dear Cuban painter-friend, decorated the house with a full-size mural on the wall of the terrace with beautiful, fantastic creatures and fishes of undersea life. He also made my full-size oil portrait with bones. I like the bones, very suiting.

My preferred relaxing place in the house is the terrace. I sit there and imagine myself in the aquarium on the wall where I swim alone with the painted colorful sea creatures. My life as a dog adopted by foreigners is great. I enjoy the cool ocean breeze and listen to cries of seagulls, songs of *'totis'* (small local blackbirds) feeding on crickets, and the noise of *'yumas'* (foreign tourists) on the beach while resting on my terrace in the shade of pine and palm trees to the soft roar of the Atlantic Ocean.

Myself, while not a tourist, I am a regular on the beach, mostly in the early mornings, to take advantage of the water being clean from polluters and the sun gentle. I also love to swim and enjoy diving because this is when I observe the morning fish hunting for food. No, I can't catch and eat fish because if I open my mouth under this disgusting salty water, it would be a very nasty burning experience. I am also prevented from barking under the water, and barking is quite essential for me when hunting, so I observe and learn about the fish and crabs while avoiding the stings of *'medusas'* (jellyfish). The *'medusa'* kiss in my snooze hurts a lot, so my rule is to avoid playing with *'medusa'*. Yes, I like eating fish, but when I am on the surface.

Here it comes from the supermarket and is mostly frozen. The local fishermen are not permitted to use anything floating for fishing; otherwise, they are prone to escape to Florida. Some rogues venture from the coastal water breakers of Malecon or on their black inner tire tubes to catch a few and sell them to tourists in Havana, but if police arrest them, they will be harshly punished because fishing activity is the priority of the state. Only the state-owned, licensed fisherman fleet is entitled to catch what is available at sea, and sell it abroad, or in hotels for the hard currency, with the rare exception of small fish products landing eventually in stores for ordinary Cubans. To sell shellfish to ordinary Cuban is illegal in Cuba because it should be sold exclusively for hard currency in hotels or abroad. Don't get the wrong impression; I am not complaining because this would constitute a crime, and in Cuba, most of all, I don't want to be characterized as conflictive. It might be the end of your carrier here. In our country, all people are divided into two categories: obedient and conflictive. I am only a modest dog - not a cat; therefore, I am obedient.

Another confession I have to make is that being brought up by this enormously powerful ocean and looking at the whole panorama from my terrace, I acquired some unjustified feelings of superiority. Some call me arrogant, not fair, but also not entirely baseless. For example, being a Cuban by birth, I can hear my human compatriots on the beach talking in their colloquial Spanish, understood only by us real Cubans. They are stalkers of *'yumas'* (foreign tourists), whom they call food. Yes, you didn't overhear me; they do call foreigners - *'la comida'* (the food) despite general knowledge that cannibals don't exist in Cuba. What my Cuban compatriots mean is that they hope to extract the food from *'yumas'* by begging or performing special services.

I love the food but don't need to beg for it from anyone. I am provided my regular meals in my own home. Sometimes, my humans even have to beg me to eat my meals, especially because I am not a big fan of cooked food containing vegetables and rice (the truth is I prefer meat and fish to everything else, much better than any foreign kibbles or canned meat, which, in any event, are not available in Cuba (even for the foreigners), or if it would have arrived at the stores for Cubans, they would be eaten straight away by the hungry Cuban humans, according to Vera.

The Atlantic Ocean is changing its colors depending on the time of day and the position of the sun: sometimes it is ultramarine green, others it is blue, but when the sun is rising or setting down, it reflects the sun and becomes gold, and sometimes dark rose and even burning gold with red. Still, most of all, I enjoy the sea breeze. It bathes me in the unique scent of the ocean world: salty, humid, pungent, cool, rich with iodine, and overpowering—very important qualities for those of us who live on this tropical island.

My little adoptive brother Cuban mix Gogi and I take our human pack to swim on the beach every day – the water is warm and very salty, but we play chasing seagulls, swimming, and diving despite the salt. All we need to do is not let the salty water into our mouths by keeping our heads high over the water when swimming and shooting our nostrils when diving.

In general, I am a good observer. I watch from our balcony when a storm is tormenting the sea, then it becomes truly angry and invades the beach with monstrous, white crest waves. Cuban stalkers and '*yumas*' have to hide away because of dangerous winds and rain, but I am safe on our terrace because it has an extended roof and strong rails. The wind bends and breaks the palm trees, flying in the air anything that was not secured, and rain lashes the ground with a vengeance.

We are leasing our house from the Cuban state company Cubanacan, which operates health tourism resorts. Health tourism in Cuban resorts is strictly prohibited for Cubans, except for Cuban elites, of course. Only foreigners and high-ranking Cuban government officials can use these facilities. One bedroom of the house on the second level is

4

for my adoptive parents and I and the rest of the house is for the office of our new Joint Venture, with the required in Cuba funny name of the International Economic Association (IEA). The other three bedrooms in our house serve as a temporary residence for our visiting foreign technical and scientific participants in IEA. They periodically arrive from distant countries, which I have never been to; they all speak English to me even though I prefer Cubano (local colloquial Spanish). You see, English is my third language, Cubano is my second, and Canine is my first.

The large office upstairs, the living room downstairs, the hall, and the dining room are the working space of our Joint Venture. Cuban law forbids foreign companies to conduct ocean surveys in Cuban territorial or economic zone waters on their own. This is why my adoptive parents, who are foreigners, were obliged to create a Cuban Joint Venture with the Cuban state. Some of the stray dogs on the beach argue with me, saying that my parents adopted me -a Cuban dog– to become registered as a Joint Venture in Cuba, but I know it is not true. These strays are envois of me. To adopt a local dog is not sufficient. My adoptive parents had to find a Cuban state company with whom they created a Joint Venture (an International Economic Association or IEA). Otherwise, they could not even lease our house in Tarara from the Cuban state. Anyway, I am proud of my local origins and feel very fortunate to belong to our mixed international human and canine pack, or the family as humans used to say.

At the time of signing the lease of our house, Tarara has not yet belonged to the Cuban military; today, they do, like the vast majority of the Cuban economy. It changed its name and became the sub-entity of CIMEX owned by the GAESA – a Cuban military conglomerate. It only shows that names and appearances in Cuba mean little. For example, the dog, which was sold as a German Sheppard guard by those people who kidnapped him from his previous owners, might be, in reality, only a sweet and noble Cuban mix scared of his own shadow. Or a small dog, after being

5

abandoned on Cuban streets, who looks like a matted, dirty skeleton rat, could, in reality, be a delicate and beautiful Pomeranian. Let me tell you my secret: the only reliable ownership in Cuba I discovered is a real bone with some meat on it. If you were lucky to get one, run and bury it deep when nobody else sees you doing it. There is no other way to protect your property.

Dora and Frank –my adoptive mommy and daddy- came a couple of years ago to Cuba at the invitation of our dear friend Comandante Tainted, who, in the opinion of many Cubans, is different from the rest of those arrogant, fossilized conformists we named in Cuba as '*comandantes botelleros*' (comandantes bottles in the rack). Dora initially met with Comandante Tainted when he was the Cuban ambassador to her country. According to her, Comandante and his family were very rare, well-meaning, good-natured, gentle survivors of that old noble bread within the Cuban revolutionary elite. Later, still being a little puppy, I met with Comandante Tainted and his family for meals at our house. I enjoyed their pleasant scent reflecting their lovely disposition and healthy vibes, especially of their teenage grandchildren: Camila and Rolandito.

In my opinion, they are attractive, modest, dignified, soft-spoken, educated, and are broadly respected by the Cuban people even today. In the past, I often took their grandchildren to the beach, where we enjoyed ourselves by playing with the ball and chasing seagulls. It has been fun, and I love their attention and rewards for catching and returning the ball. Even though personally, I don't understand why humans like bouncing the ball around, I would rather run with it as fast as I can, just to see who can catch me. That is because I know who will win the game, ja, ja. Nobody ever could catch me when I run hard unless with a motor vehicle.

According to my adoptive parents, Comandante Tainted sent an official mail with an invitation to my Mommy Dora when he returned to Cuba from his posting abroad. He described in his mail how the new Cuban law provided numerous opportunities for foreign investors in Cuba and how Cuba desperately needs but lacks those new skills and survey technologies, which Mommy Dora recently presented at the International Offshore Survey conference attended by him and the Cuban science attaché. Mommy Dora said she remembered this distinguished gentleman and his family from the meetings with him at the conference, and she replied to his kind invitation. It was not difficult to convince her husband Frank during the winter season to accompany her to a tropical country to investigate the opportunities in deep-sea exploration and recovery.

By that time, due to his sympathies with Soviet *perestroika*, our Comandante Tainted already lost all his favors with Fidel Castro, who abhorred *perestroika,* and Comandante Tainted was discharged from his ministry, initially into a '*pajama plan'* (at home in pajamas), but later was given a new impossible mission by Fidel Castro to find the lost ancient treasures from the sunken Spanish galleons hidden in coastal deep water and caves of the most remote and undeveloped region of Cuba: Guanahabibes. Possibly, this was done to remove him from the Center of Power at a safe distance because he was dangerously popular. In my opinion, just like in the case of canines: the good-natured dog has no chance in a dog fight. The best that Comandante Tainted could aspire to was to be extricated from the dog fight.

Obviously, dogfighting wasn't his forte, but he was a survivor, and as my Daddy Frank used to say, he found comfort in displaying the classic case of cognitive dissonance syndrome. My daddy Frank is a psychologist, and the terms he is using are difficult to understand, especially in the case of a canine interlocutor. Basically, in our canine language, it means total submission to your abusers by believing that their abuse is for your own good because you already invested in your relationship with them and now totally depend on your abusers. You want to think that the abusers are always right, and to strengthen this belief; you join the pack of abusers with maximum enthusiasm. They always use this technique in training dogfighters. I wasn't trained as a dogfighter, but I understand what it takes.

Still, Comandante Tainted arranged for my adoptive parents a compatible Cuban partner, a Cuban company Carisub – the only Cuban commercial company originally permitted to work in marine archeological search and recovery. Dora and Frank were happy to create a Joint Venture with this company. Carisub used human divers operating from their small yachts. My adoptive parents offered to improve their operations by using the latest survey technology from the large ship to work in deep water. I enjoyed the visits of Nelson, Carisub's young, cheerful, confident, and good-looking director when he was coming over to work with us in our office. He always brought with him Guapo – his one-year-old German shepherd puppy. While Guapo and I were playing on the beach with seagulls and diving to scare the fish, our humans were working on their four-year business plan required to register our International Economic Association (IEA).

At the time, all our friends: foreign and Cuban, anticipated that Cuba would begin to introduce gradual changes into a more open democratic society, like other previous Soviet satellites in the preceding period. In the 90th after Soviet perestroika, they felt enthusiastic about participating in such a historical event. This belief led my adoptive parents, their friends, and their families to invest in Cuban undertaking hoping for fascinating new opportunities to open in Cuba with international scientific collaboration. To expedite this new liberating undertaking was their main motivation. They wanted to be early on the ground of this paradise island for such an opening.

Built on a hill facing the Atlantic Ocean, the town of Tarara is a fast and easy trip from Havana and the international airport, with newly paved highways going directly to this previously private cottage residence of wealthy Habaneros. During the pre-revolutionary years, the dogs of Tarara lived in their homes with their human families. After the victory of the revolution, these families were regarded by the revolutionaries as the *bourgeoisie,* and the Cuban revolutionary government confiscated their private properties on the beach, forcing them to leave the country and abandon their dogs in Cuba, which became homeless. They and their descendants unprotected from the street romantic aggression of strays became chaotically mixed breeds in a matter of few years.

The new revolutionary families, such as Che Guevara's, and Soviet senior officials, moved into those houses. Che Guevara even built his own huge and, in my view, very ugly building occupying the whole block in Tarara for the school of PNR, Policia Nacional Revolucionaria (National Revolutionary Police) – Internal Affairs Law Enforcement Forces (criminal and political). All this new development was only for humans; there was nothing for dogs.

Original houses in Tarara serving their main function of beach cottages were built of concrete and hardly could be compared to the luxurious stone residences expropriated from the rich in Havana. For this reason, the majority of the new revolutionary elite occupied the mansions in Havana. Later for a couple of years, some of the vacant Tarara's housing, those which were further removed from the sea, became a health resort for revolutionary pioneers: Cuban and later Ukrainian children affected by the Chernobyl nuclear disaster.

Still, only a few of these houses occupied by the new elite were looked after, the rest got trashed, and their contents were stolen. In my opinion, the Cuban government would benefit more if they would house the abandoned dogs of Tarara in those empty houses instead of sending Zoonosis to catch and assassinate them. What is Zoonosis, and what it does, I will tell you later. For now, let me tell you why I believe that the strays of Tarara could have solved the embezzlement problem in the abandoned houses. If the administrators had allowed the abandoned dogs to stay in houses they lived in before, dogs would be happy to repay the favor by working as guards. Their service would be much cheaper than those of human guards, who steal everything. Dogs would guard their houses only for their food and water, but nobody thought of this brilliant idea or asked my advice.

As I said, lacking proper security and maintenance, the majority of these beautiful houses in Tarara came into total disrepair during their long-term misuse. For this reason, after the Soviets stopped heavy subsidies to Cuba in the early 90th, the Cuban government experienced its first severe economic crisis, *'periodo especial'* (special period). They legalized foreign tourism and limited foreign investment in Cuba to prevent the socio-economic crash. A new, hard currency health resort in Tarara, exclusively for foreign clients and high-ranking government officials, was initially managed by the Cubanacan state tourism commercial conglomerate. The main rationale was the convenience of long-term hard-currency leasing to foreign accredited companies and embassies. In addition to the long lease payments for these houses and cottages on the beach, the foreign or JV companies paid for all required renovations and created significant hard currency income for the government. This is how my adoptive parents came to lease the house in Tarara from Cubanacan, who were at those times known as nice, dog-tolerant people and later became my friends.

While in Cuba, we were fortunate to form excellent relationships with many other friendly, intelligent, soft-spoken, and modest Cubans: scientists and managers. I, in particular, enjoyed getting together with them for snacks or meals on our terrace overlooking the sea and the beach. Everyone was loving me and acted generously with their food - a real paradise for me, you may say. I am a very observant dog and learned from my numerous, enthusiastic teachers many tricks. I must admit, I felt important, if not at the center of the universe, then at least the center of Tarara, because the members of my human pack played with me and spoke to me all day long in both languages: English and Spanish.

My teachers told me repeatedly that I am a truly fortunate Doberman: smart with an exceptionally good sense of smell, an amazing athlete, grown tall with a broad and powerful chest, strong elongated muscles, light-footed, graceful gait, wearing a sleek, shiny chocolate coat. In the very worst case, they told me, I could aspire to become a movie actor. I do not know about that because I prefer staying with my human and canine pack in our house on our beach. To tell you honestly, I am disgusted with the images of ears and tails mutilated Dobermans in films and the myth created by the hostile portrayal of our breed.

I attended the classes in a Cuban fishing research ship, leased by my adoptive parents in Cuba and outfitted in a Cuban shipyard with the latest European deep-water marine bottom survey and communications equipment. European and Canadian technical personnel came to Cuba to train Cuban scientists and engineers to operate the latest survey equipment. I shall confess, it is tough to work on the board of the ship at sea during the stormy weather, to maintain a balance on the ship's deck, without puking, but it is even more challenging to climb up and get down the short but steep ship ladders. It was really hard and took a lot of learning, but I will talk about that later.

As I mentioned before, I always liked Comandante Tainted - this tall, slim, soft, slow-spoken, very distinguished gentleman with delicate and kind facial features and softly curled thick white hair. He is always modestly but elegantly dressed and smelling of good talc lemon powder - my preferable talc power. I loved to sniff his crispy-starched ironed *guayabera* and well-polished shoes. He knows I like to show off with him. Who wouldn't? He is such an important and distinguished man! Sometimes, I feel tempted to show him how tall and strong I became. That is when I stand on my hind legs, the way humans do. Don't take it wrong; I know with whom I can and with whom I should not compete. Don't you worry, I am not stupid and know who is the highest Alpha. Usually, I never jump on his shoulders to hug him unless he invites me so. I always act polite and respectful. Why not, if it helps him feel generous in sharing with me his appetizers?

This time, I was told to control my enthusiasm during this meeting with our influential friends, for they might be instrumental, according to Dora, in removing the sudden severe threat in which I found myself unexpectedly due to being reported to Zoonosis as a dangerous dog. The vicious enemy made this ridiculous, totally unfair accusation against me. I perceived his murderous intentions ten or five minutes before he arrived, thanks to my canine precognition, which humans call ESP.

Usually, I am an amiable social being and enjoy the company of our visitors, and I was trained not to bark or jump at them in excitement. I greeted our visitors sitting on my hind legs and smiling with my ears relaxed, and pushed back, but in this case, I had to fulfill my mission of protector and warn my pack that the enemy with murderous intention was coming. When I felt that our enemy was approaching, I decided to protect the entrance door and started barking. Diego did not understand my message and not reacted correctly, obliging me to start hyper-barking and jumping at the entrance door to scare the approaching enemy.

I succeeded in scaring him, but Diego dragged me away to the backyard. Would you call me a dangerous dog, or would you rather admire my clairvoyant talent and loyal disposition after that? Diego is my instructor and dear friend. He is also our Toyota van driver. Normally, I obey his orders, not because I am afraid of him, but because I love him and want to please him. Despite being a low-ranking, middle-aged, soft-spoken, sweet Cuban guy, he knows everybody everywhere in Havana and across Cuba. He is kind, handsome, masterful, and handy - a supper guy in my eyes. I trust him entirely, except this time when the dark cloud of premonition came all over me, warming me of the approach by the enemy of our pack. I was doing my best to alarm Diego, but he didn't understand and dragged me away into the backyard. Later he even scolded me and threatened me with Zoonosis.

Chapter 2

Zoonosis, whose long name is Canine Observation Center, is a truly vicious state company operating by the Cuban government across the island in all Cuban cities. They kidnap and assassinate my canine brothers on the pretense of taking care of their health. Their wretched canine victims are usually captured while playing on streets, parks, beaches, or even in their houses' front or back yards. The official rules are that after seventy-two hours of being kept without water or food in the cages of Zoonosis, all these kidnapped puppies will be killed. That being said, according to the rumors, due to the limited space in prison cages, in practice, these pups are exterminated in less than forty-eight hours. Only those pups whose owners have discovered where their pups were taken, where they were taken, and those who have the money to pay the ransom for the release of their pups and have the transportation to arrive at the remote location of Zoonosis before the forty-eight hours, will be spared. Zoonosis, as it claims, will take the health care of the rest of the kidnapped pups by assassinating them with the sharp but cheap lethal-dose poison of strychnine - a long and tortuous way to die.

Diego was right. Zoonosis with their murderous wagon already came last week to arrest me, but my family pack was warned of the danger by Fernando – the manager of Tarara and my good friend. This permitted my family pack to hide my younger adopted brother Gogi and me in the secret underground concrete bunker of Carlos Prío

Socarrás. Frustrated about not finding me, Zoonosis kidnapped all other dogs they could find in Tarara.

Now I feel terribly guilty and persecuted. Because I was the one who was denounced as a dangerous dog, but I survived, all the other dogs of Tarara were snatched by Zoonosis. They had to pay with their lives for my reaction to the enemy. If Zoonosis catches me, they will kill me straight away, according to Cuban law. Is this fair? I am still only a pup! I am not dangerous; I was only warning the enemy that I protected my pack and my house. Ask anyone, and they will tell you that I am a loving and genuinely cuddly pup, simply trying to be helpful.

But let us return to the visit of our distinguished guests Comandante Tainted and his family: Maria, wife of Comandante Tainted – a beautiful, flower-scented, older lady with her freshly done hairdo, dressed in a modest formal dress, wearing heels, even just for this informal visit to the beach, and Camila, their sweet, slim, and cheeky, teenaged blond granddaughter. They wanted me to take them to the beach, where they would swim and laugh, watching me chase the seagulls. No such luck. This time I was not allowed to accompany them to the beach. Mommy Dora apologized to her visitors by explaining that I was unfairly denounced to Zoonosis as a dangerous dog and would be euphonized if Zoonosis caught me. She recounted how Zoonosis recently arrived and snatched all dogs they found in Tarara, independent of their breed or color.

In my humble opinion, what is taking place is incredibly unfair! The little stray '*mulaticas*' (colored) Cuban girls '*luchadoras* or *jineteras*' (hookers), who, according to my Mommy Dora, despite their tender young age (between 11 and 16), are very dangerous because of infections, are allowed to continue hunting for the foreign tourists on the beach unmolested, but we, the dogs of Tarara, are eliminated from the beach in this resort town.

This was even worse now than during Hurricane Irene, which attacked Tarara with the force of hurricane three this year. Then, we lost all electricity and communications. The wind was so strong and noisy that it filled me and my adopted brother Gogi with terror, and it broke many roofs and palm trees in Tarara. The ocean roar was so loud and powerful that I was afraid the ocean might attack and swallow our house. All of the houses in Tarara got inundated through the night with rainfall resembling a waterfall. We attempted to protect our huge glass windows with duct tape – a poor joke. The flying palm trees and debris could break our full-size window walls without effort. But we got lucky.

The wind blew and beat the debris against the roofs of our neighbors instead. I was helping my adoptive parents remove the water from the inundated bedrooms by attaching myself to their legs while they were removing the buckets with water using the mop through the night. I must admit, my tail being hidden between my paws made it clear how much I was scared, but nothing like my little adopted brother puppy Gogi and his mother Pretty – a small stray blond canine tramp from the beach. Both of them were hiding on top of the sofas of our office under the pillows. Hurricane Irene was stationary and lasted full three days, but nobody was hurt and, even the stray dogs somehow survived this horror. I suspect that the locals sheltered the wretched poor strays in neighboring towns.

As soon as the hurricane moves away, everybody came out from their hiding to scavenge for some food. The stray dogs of Tarara got lucky. Fernando, a well-natured Cuban manager of Tarara's resort, brought from the resort's restaurant for them a large number of beefsteaks that became defrosted due to the lack of electricity, and being afraid to offer possibly contaminated beefsteaks to humans, he gave them to the stray dogs of Tarara. What happened last week was very different. Fernando suddenly appeared at our door to warn us, "Zoonosis just called me and said it is sending their death wagon from Havana. They are coming to Tarara due to a complaint about Benz acting as a dangerous dog."

As a result, Gogi and I were immediately hidden from Zoonosis by our human pack. The rest of the dogs and strays of Tarara, who didn't benefit from this preventive warning, were savagely hunted by the brutes of Zoonosis with long snare poles that arrived before my humans could run to find them on the beach or warn other dog owners.

None of the kidnapped dogs were later released; they were all murdered. Never again did we see our little blond stray Pretty (mother of Gogi). She was always running with her stray canine gang somewhere on the beach. Poor Pretty obviously fell their victim. Mommy Dora traveled the next day to the location of Zoonosis in the municipality of La Lisa, but when she arrived there, she was denied the information about Pretty. The clerk of Zoonosis said that they didn't register dogs arriving that day and therefore could not find Pretty, even if they wanted to.

"Lies, lies, and more lies. Probably, I already came late," said Mommy Dora, "because the office of Zoonosis would open only the next morning and, probably, Zoonosis had to fulfill their daily required minimum number of pups to kill the previous day when they raided Tarara."

Still, Zoonosis hadn't fulfilled their mandate of killing the dangerous Doberman Benz; it was not happy about the results of their raid; it might return any moment to Tarara looking for me. For this reason, Gogi and I had to continue hiding every day in the underground bunker of Carlos Prío Socarrás, which we hated. Every day, except today, because, according to my Mommy, "today we are protected," she said, "Comandante Tainted, would not allow anyone to take you away in his presence."

Today was another gorgeous Sunday – perfect for my outing with our female visitors to spend on the beach, but these lovely ladies had to leave for a short swim on their own, without me, while we sat down with Comandante

Tainted in our living room to explain him the reason for this awful situation.

Mommy Dora described to Comandante Tainted how the Cuban military suddenly took over our International Economic Association (IEA) and how the new Cuban boss, Colonel Beltran, suddenly replaced our previous Cuban partner in IEA, and why Colonel Beltran branded me a 'dangerous dog' just for my barking at him. Mommy Dora described how Zoonosis arrived to execute the order to arrest a dangerous dog Dobermann Benz to euthanize him immediately upon his arrest according to Cuban law.

While my adoptive parents were relaying this menacing story, I demonstrated my noble character by laying on my back beside the seat of Comandante, with my trout and genitals exposed for biting, should Comandante wish to do so. In our dog language, it means the ultimate submission. How could anyone think that I am a 'dangerous dog' when I submit with such pleasure to my dear friends and protectors.

Comandante Tainted was shocked by the story. "This is outrageous," he said to his wife when she returned from the beach.

"What can we do? The military is just too powerful in our country. It would make no good to complain about Colonel to his superiors," she replied.

"I am thinking about a different approach," interrupted Mommy Dora cautiously. "You mentioned before that the metal detectors used by you previously didn't have the power needed for finding gold and silver. You inquired if our magnetometer is more powerful than the metal detectors used by you in search of gold and silver objects hidden in the caves of Guanahacabibes."

"Yes, Dora. I am afraid this might be what we will really need if we want to succeed," answered Comandante Tainted.

Why all this talk about metal detectors and magnetometers? Shouldn't they better discuss my fate? I thought, concerned.

"Well, I am not so sure if this is what you need. While it is true that our marine magnetometer is much more powerful, I am sorry to disappoint you; it is not the right instrument for the job in the caves. Our marine magnetometer is a fish-type, deep-water instrument towed at least two and a half ship lengths behind the ship to assure that the ship's magnetic field will not interfere with the measurements of magnetization caused by the presence of ferrous iron – usually steel-made shipwrecks on the deep ocean bottom, not the diamagnetic metals, such as gold and silver," she said.

"Our experts told me that it is simply a matter of power and exact positioning," replied confused Comandante Tainted.

"Diamagnetic metals, such as copper, gold, and silver," Mommy Dora continued, "repel the magnet, and for these metals, you would need a metal detector of much higher frequency."

"What you mean, higher frequency?" asked the puzzled comandante.

"Frequency is the number of electronic waves that the machine will send into the ground. The higher frequency signals would need a higher power. Still, it is not so simple. The size, shape, and distance from a target, along with other environmental variables, affect the accuracy of the detector," replied Mommy Dora.

"Are these types of metal detectors currently available?" asked Maria.

"There are no commercially available metal detectors that allow changing the frequency and size of coils on the spot during the search," said Mommy Dora.

"Another factor is the condition of the ground itself. The frequency measured in the ground high in moisture and salt content can be quite incorrect. Therefore, the task of searching for gold and silver underground in the caves of Guanahacabibes is an extremely complex and uncertain undertaking. We invited you today to suggest non-technical means in search of gold and silver. Have you heard about the ore-sniffing dogs used to find gold and silver under the ground and even underwater?" asked Daddy Frank.

"I heart of tracking hunting dogs," wondered surprised comandante, "what are those ore-sniffing dogs?"

"These are the dogs trained to find all sorts of sulfide ore and pyrite ore: gold ore, arsenian pyrite, zinc, copper, silver, or nickel. Dogs could be trained to track and find the odor of mineral ores by their scend. Humans can't detect these scents, but dogs can. Scents mean everything to dogs. I can say that dog is a snout with a body attached," answered Mommy Dora.

"In fact, dogs also have what is called a vomeronasal organ, Jacobson's organ, that functions as a second nose. This is part of a dog's accessory olfactory system. A dog's olfactory cortex is part of its brain. It is about forty times larger in dogs than in humans, and about thirty-five percent of a dog's brain deals with odors, while only five percent of a human brain is devoted to smell. Dogs can use each nostril separately to increase their smelling abilities further. The snout of a dog is about a million times more sensitive than that of a human, depending on their particular breed," added Daddy Frank.

WOW, I thought, a *million times more sensitive*, f*abulous! This is why I am so talented. Daddy always knows the best! His brain is like a Wikipedia. That's why we formed a mutual admiration society. We would do anything it takes to protect our human and canine packs.*

"Benz could be just such a dog," suggested Daddy Frank in sync with me. "Look at his superlong Dobermans' snout.

The longer their snout is, the larger the olfactory system it has. Benz could serve you as an ore-sniffing dog. He could be useful in locating those lost treasures. I read about such teams composed of geologists and dogs in Finland, Russia, and Sweden dedicated to searching the underground and even the underwater ore."

"Why shouldn't we try to do the same with Benz in Guanahacabibes? The appropriate training could improve his natural talents in finding objects under the ground. He is available if you wish to appoint him for the position of treasure-searcher in your team. His talents might save our IEA from the current obstacles and hostilities. If he succeeds, his status, and therefore the status of our IEA in Cuba, will immediately change for the Cuban national economy. Can we show you his talents just for the sake of demonstration?" asked Mommy Dora.

"Well, we have some new developments in my project," warily responded comandante. "That changes our project in caves substantially, but yours is an interesting idea. I don't know much about canine sensors in finding treasures, but I am convinced Benz could locate snakes and poisonous spiders in caves. *'Palante muestralo'* (Go ahead)," reasoned Comandante Tainted.

Mommy Dora removed her golden earrings and gave them to Camila, the granddaughter of Comandante Tainted. She said, "Let's play this game with Benz. It will be fast, I promise. You and Diego, please go outside into the backyard. Diego, our Cuban driver, will dig the ground in a location of your choice to hide my earring, Camila, and when the buried earring is completely hidden, we will ask Benz to find it, ok?"

Mommy must be joking, I thought. *We rehearsed this before, and she knows it is not a challenge for me. She also knows that her earring has her scent, and this makes my task easy. I really want to show off to these important visitors. Why doesn't she ask me to find something more spectacular, like the earrings of Camila, which I smell are hidden in her pocket? Her grandparents probably don't want her to wear golden non-proletarian earrings, which is why she is hiding them.*

I pointed with my snout to Camila's pocket and wagged my tail as a sign for Mommy Dora about this more interesting demonstration, but Mommy Dora didn't understand my signs. She sent Diego and Camila to the backyard garden while we were waiting in the dining room. When finally, after sniffing Dora's other earring, I was allowed into our fenced backyard garden. My snout let me straight away to the scent of the earring freshly dug into the ground. Too easy, in my humble opinion, but instead of complaining, I proudly demonstrated my newly learned skill in announcing find: to sit in the position of a good dog beside the find, my ears up and barking while looking at the audience. My audience burst into applause, which culminated in a substantial meat reward from the kitchen table.

Is this what you call ore-dog? It is easy and well-rewarded. In such a case, I am ready, I thought and felt even more confident of my talents, but Dora continued promising to Comandante that I will get additional training to upgrade and specialize my ore-searching skills if he approves my appointment of a treasure-search dog in his team.

After finishing this insightful discussion about my talents, we commenced the most important activity of the day: eating in the dining room. My tactical position under the dining table offered the advantage of receiving meat morsels from everyone who admires and supports my talents. The females are usually my best contributors; it must be their maternal instinct, so I always stay by their legs under the table, just if they will have the urge to share their delicious cheesy arancini veal steak with me; this is what they called the main plate. Its smell drives me crazy, but Mommy Dora taught me to show my good manners to these important guests. *Clearly, the females are more appreciative of my refined talents, for they are better at sending large veal pieces my way.*

After the main course, while seeping his wine Comandante Tainted said, "I understand that the change of Cuban partner in your IEA is a difficult experience for you, but the military in Cuba is extremely powerful. If they made this decision, nothing could be done. I only can advise you to adapt."

"Our difficulties are serious, Comandante since Colonel Beltran wants to replace our Cuban technical personnel, whom we have already trained, with his own employees," answered Mommy Dora in a low somber voice. "For a reason unknown to us, our previous Cuban director Nelson has completely disappeared. Nobody knows where he is, and the military overtaking would now delay the start of our ocean exploration. We would have to commence training of new military personnel from the very beginning. Colonel Beltran also wants to charge a larger salary payment for his people despite their lack of qualifications. Deep-water exploration requires highly qualified technical and scientific expertise, and Colonel Beltran doesn't appreciate it. Our budget is modest, and his intervention will ruin our whole undertaking before we started the actual work."

"I don't have the power to oppose the decision of military leadership, Dora; it is much above me, you understand?" answered Comandante Tainted, looking worried after exchanging looks with his wife after a long silence.

"What I don't understand," continued arguing Mommy Dora, "which is the law that permits the Cuban military to overtake our International Economic Association by replacing the Cuban partner without consulting with us? Is there any internationally recognized commercial law permitting that?"

"I am sorry, Dora, but it is given that in Cuba, you are working under Cuban law, not international law. All Cuban marine activities must be approved by the Cuban military, which is not functioning according to commercial laws; they are their own law. There is nothing anyone can do to change their decision. Couldn't you somehow adapt to your new partner?" he suggested in a conciliatory, apologetic, and somber voice.

He was sad, and I felt sorry for him. *This is the moment when he needs my support*, I thought. I decided to move under the table by him and show him my sincere compassion. *O, Comandante, let me lick your shoes, don't be sad, and please consider me for any opening in your cave treasure-hunting adventure.*

"Stop licking my shoes under the table Benz!" Comandante Tainted protested, annoyed with my diplomatic platitudes. "I didn't forget about you," and he dropped another meat morsel for me.

"Do you think we could raise the matter of military takeover over our Joint Venture in Cuban courts?" Daddy Frank asked naively.

"You could," replied Comandante Tainted, "but I sincerely don't advise you. Only the ultimate authority of Fidel could change the decision of the military. Maybe you should employ a different strategy instead of a legal challenge. I think you might be right about our need for a treasure-search dog in our mandate assigned by Fidel himself."

Chapter 3

"Please tell us more, Comandante, if you can, about those new developments in your treasure search project," inquired Daddy Frank.

"Well, you probably remember the legend of the hidden treasures of the Cathedral of Merida?" asked Comandante. "Maybe you are right by suggesting that Benz could help us. If only your equipment or your dog could assist us in locating the treasures in the caves of Guanacabibes, this would justify my addressing your concerns with Fidel himself."

"Good idea, Comandante. Could you please update us about new developments in your project?" insisted Daddy Frank.

"' *Bueno, la cosa es'* (Well, the matter is)*,* as I mentioned before, on orders from our Comandante en Jefe Fidel Castro, we commissioned the study by a professional team of Cuban historians and anthropologists of archival data about these hidden treasures in the caves of Guanahacabibes. The whole story is about the early days of the conquest of Mexico and the treasures kept in the Cathedral of San Ildefonso in the city of Merida in Yucatan, the first and oldest cathedral in Mexico.

"After the death of Arzobispo of Yucatan, known as a defender of natives in 1636, the Vatican found themselves in a contentious relationship with the Spanish Governor of Yucatan of the period Marques de Santo Flora. Marques ruled Yucatan by oppression, committing serious abuses on the enslaved Mayan population, provoking their constant rebellion. Keep in mind that Yucatan pertained to the Spanish Empire in the XVII century and not to Mexico."

"O, so it is a product of a conflict between the natives, the Governor, and the Vatican? Tell us more," implored Dora.

"In those early days of Conquest, most Indians of Yucatan still longed for the time before the arrival of Spaniards, and their uprisings presented serious threats to Spanish rule in Mexico. The Franciscans, led by Fray Diego de Landa, destroyed all the Mayan codices – Mayan scripted history. They tortured and killed a large number of Mayan natives who did not relinquish their own religious beliefs. Both Catholic orders: the Franciscans and Jesuits, were competing for the converted native souls. This produced even more friction between all groups," said comandante.

"Sounds like a modern Mexico. Everyone is complaining about their level of violence. Many groups, including the European Catholic church, constantly fighting for power," said Frank.

"The brutal Spanish Governor Diego Zapata de Cardenas (marques of Santo Floro) declared war on indigenous Maya in Balacar (called Riviera Maya today) and burned their towns and cities, desecrated their temples. The natives dispersed into the surrounding forests. During these disturbances, the Catholic clerics in Yucatan evacuated in secret the precious valuables from their own churches before the anticipated attacks of natives. For a good reason - the origin of these valuables were tributes and donations to the Catholic churches collected from natives across Yucatan," explained Comandante.

"How many churches were in Yucatan of that period?" asked Frank.

"Colonial society was complex; it was a caste society," answered Maria. The Episcopal city was divided into parishes, which implied a racial division: one for Spanish or white; one for blacks and browns; one for the Indians servants of Spaniards; and one for all other Indians. Later it was moved to the "Episcopal City" under its jurisdiction of 12 churches and chapels. Still, constant insecurity obliged the clerics to store the church valuables in The Cathedral of San Ildefonso of the city of Merida, for it was regarded as the best-protected stronghold. Meanwhile, the coastal areas of the Peninsula lacked the defense and were sparsely populated, permitting the English loggers to settle in Cape Catochi and Cozumel Island illegally, which became the base for pirates by the mid-17th century."

"Are you saying that the early pirates from Cozumel and Catochi raided Merida despite its distance from the coast? Is there a record of that?" asked Frank surprised.

"No, at that early time, it was only a serious treat. When new Archbishop Fray Juan Alonzo y Ocon arrived at Merida in 1638 to take the seat of Yucatan, he found himself amid a conflict between the Governor of Yucatan Diego Zapata de Cardenas with natives, as well as with French, English, and Dutch insurgents. In March 1640, Merida panicked when news came that Dutch pirates had landed in the port of Sisal and were preparing to reach Merida - the provincial capital," said Maria. As a result, the interior of Yucatan clashed in the war between rebel natives and the Governor's troops while pirates threatened the undefended coast. Archbishop felt, and it became too dangerous to hide the treasures in the secret storage of the Cathedral of San Ildefonso."

"It is getting warmer, Comandante. Clashes and constant wars in Mexico, including Yucatan, continued throughout its history. This is how the Mayan civilization came into decay even before the Spanish conquest, and it hasn't stopped yet," commented Frank.

"The Archbishop also got into serious problems with the governor Diego Zapata," continued Comandante, "so much that Diego Zapata was temporarily excommunicated and replaced by Don Luis de Céspedes, who also had serious differences with the Archbishop. Finally, the secret envoy of the Vatican was sent to Archbishop de Habana with a proposition to secretly ship these treasures to Cuba for their safekeeping until such a moment that treasures could be returned to the Vatican. The deal was granted, and three Spanish vessels were secretly contracted in the spring of 1642 to ship these treasures from their storage in The Cathedral of San Ildefonso of Merida to Havana. I repeat in secret because of the fear that either the Spanish Governor or the warring native tribes, or the pirates would attempt to appropriate these iconoclastic treasures."

"When in the August of 1642 small squadron, consisting of three Spanish vessels, left from the Northern-Eastern coast of Yucatan from the point between Sisal and Chubuma, they discovered that they were followed by *'bajeles'* (the pirate ships) from Cape Catochi. Sailing at full speed on its way to Havana to escape the pirates, this small squadron approached the dangerous Cabo de San Antonio (Cape of San Antonio), the western end of Cuba, which as you know, borders the Yucatan Strait, leaving a difficult passage, where many ships sunk those times due to strong current of Gulf Stream," said Maria.

"The bajeles with pirates," she continued, "were chasing them closely for several days, fast approaching them near Cabo de San Antonio. It would be a matter of hours before the fastest pirate ship would reach the Galleon "Princesa de Toledo" carrying treasure, which was detained by the impetuous waters of the Yucatan Strait. The four friers (Catholic ordained priests) from the Cathedral of San Ildefonso, who were in charge of safekeeping treasure, decided not to risk the valuable treasures in battle with pirates and hide them in the caves of Cabo de San Antonio (Cape of San Antonio) until the end of the conflict. The treasure of incalculable value consisted of a large volume of massive gold, golden disks, bars, coins, and religious native jewelry.

"I hope you got the list and some description of this treasure. That might be helpful. Do you know what happened next?" asked Frank.

"The sailors and friars unloaded the treasure on the beach, found the nearby cave, and hid it there. They marked the location of the cavern and drew a map of where it was. After that, the Spanish marines returned to their ship to join the other two Spanish ships in the fight with the pirates. Meanwhile, the friars hid the treasures deeper inside the cavern. After waiting for five days for the return of the marines, they decided to leave the cavern and search for help because their food and water became depleted, for they haven't anticipated such a long wait for the return of the marines. They left the cavern to ask for help by walking across the peninsula of Guanahacabibes towards the town of Guane (then called Nueva Filipina) located in the center of Pinar del Rio at a distance of twenty-three kilometers from the peninsular coast," said Comandante Tainted.

"There were no roads to the interior of the peninsula – only the sharp as knife eroded limestone formations called 'seboruco' or 'dientes del perro' (teeth of a dog) – the fractured formations of limestone with large sharp knife edges and vicious thorns growing between these formations rendering the area being impenetrable without specially reinforced boots. The only mode of transport between various locations of the north and south coast of the peninsula in those times was by the sea in a boat since the interior of the peninsula was a deadly territory for more than one league (5.6 kilometers)."

"I understand that the coastal ground of the peninsula is all naked karst and mangroves. Karst is the limestone eroded by dissolution, producing caves, sinkholes, and ridges. Not just the peninsula of Guanahacabibes, but the whole province of Pinar del Rio is still sparsely populated, despite your good efforts in building a current road connecting it to Havana. To reach the town of Guane, these Mexican friers would have to walk for weeks over the sharp karst!" exclaimed Daddy Frank.

"Indeed, out of four friars - only one, the youngest of them -, blood-mix mestizo finally managed to reach the fences of small-town Guane. The other three, without water or food, wearing Mexican sandals instead of specially reinforced boots, have died from thirst, hunger, and exhaustion. The mestizo was found and brought in a state of near death to the only church existing in Guanahacabibes at the time. That is where he made his testimony to the priest of the Church of Guane before he died from exhaustion," answered Comandante.

"I hope that the priest of the Church of Guane kept the original records," said Frank.

"It was said that a bit later, the priest of that Church of Guane disappeared," said Maria, "and nobody could find him again. Volume 1 of this church's Parish Register Death Book had this story recorded with the names and other details of the deceased Spanish friar who gave the testimony. Again, strangely enough, Volumes 1 and 2 of the church registers also disappeared; only Volume 3 is still available. The Church itself was moved and rebuilt in different locations twice. It is curious that in the early nineteenth century, the Vatican purchased large land properties in Guanahacabibes. Undoubtedly something rare, considering that it was an almost uninhabited area without roads or communication. An alleged envoy of the Vatican arrived at Guanahacabibes in the early twentieth century. He made several forays into the interior of the territory. It has been said that he was some kind of special agent, who mastered several languages and martial arts and came on a secret mission to secure the treasure."

"Recently, our *Comandante en Jefe* Fidel Castro," interjected Comandante Tainted, "personally assigned me to investigate and to locate these lost treasures, which value would make an important contribution to our economy. My task was difficult since the map with the cave's location with hidden treasures and the testimony of the Spanish priest were not available. Twice I organized the cavern expeditions carried out with the help of our arm forces equipped with metal detectors, but after extensive and detailed search, we only attained to destroy the largest cavern of the coastal cave network, which extends everywhere; across and along our porous limestone peninsula of Guanahabibes."

"Comandante, we heard from your office about the use of dynamite in caverns by the Cuban army and a consequent collapse of the ceiling in the largest of the cave of that network, which was known as Cueva de Los Musulmanos, is it correct?"- asked Dora.

"Yes, various expeditions took place, but nothing of significance was found. Our major achievement, of which we are very proud, was that Guanahacabibes, specifically in Cape San Antonio, being the island's westernmost point, has been declared a National Park and Biosphere Reserve by UNESCO in 1987. It is geologically different from the rest of the island. I mean that geologically it is part of the karst of Yucatan and not of Cuba. This is very important, and we decided to inquire the Vatican if they had any available information on this matter. Their reply took a long time, but recently their envoy came to Cuba offering to cooperate with us in the recovery."

"O, really? This is a very important new development!" reacted Daddy Frank.

"Yes, I will have to discuss your ideas with the envoy of the Vatican, meanwhile start training Benz in finding gold and silver. He might become our new member of the next search expedition."

Chapter 4

The life of a Doberman could be in constant peril thanks to the idiotic myth and lies people invent about Doberman bread and their unexplainable hate of Jews and blacks. I can't understand how Doberman dogs are expected to recognize who is a Jew and who is a Catholic. I am convinced that if any dog behaves aggressively, it is because he/she was trained to be aggressive. The guilty are those imbecile human trainers who force their dogs to attack other people. We dogs learn, just like human children do, from our teachers and the environment. I was never trained to attack, neither a person nor a fly. I play with and love all people, animals, and even birds, except when I have a premonition about someone coming to hurt my pack. That is because I do have a very strong pack protection instinct, and I expect the same from all responsible members of my pack. To me, there is just nothing more important than the safety of my pack, and I am willing to give my life for it.

The life of a Doberman denounced as a dangerous dog, who is now on the persecution blacklist of Zoonosis, is true torture. Fernando - my friend and the manager of Tarara, warned daddy that Zoonosis would not stop hunting for me until it catches me. They don't trust Fernando anymore, and they are planning a new ambush aimed to capture me in surprise without a previous warning from the management of Tarara. This is why Gogi and I became prisoners inside the secret underground bunker of ex-Cuban President

Carlos Prío Socarrás. We were told it was for our own safety.

The underground bunker has no windows, and its meter-thick concrete walls could assure that our barks, cries, and pleadings are left unheard by our neighbors in Tarara, who might denounce our hiding place if and when Zoonosis will arrive in ambush. The air in the bunker is stale; despite the ventilator, it is very hot inside, with nothing to do all day long, regardless of our toys being brought there for us. The only relief is at night when we are allowed into the backyard garden to do our essentials. After that, we are led into our bedroom with Mommy Dora and Daddy Frank, who had to compensate for our sufferings with the special treats and massages, we like, especially under the snout and underbelly. We are the members of their family; this is why we must sleep together protecting each other.

We could see that Mommy Dora and Daddy Frank have also suffered from having to imprison us in the bunker, but it is not enough for our consolation. By seven o'clock in the morning, we are yanked from our bed to the backyard for our business and then led into the bunker for the whole day. Sure thing, we have plenty of water and food inside the bunker, but the life of a dog is much more than the food. We felt imprisoned, deprived of freedom, sick of boredom, and lonely. In our opinion, there is nothing worse than losing freedom, and being locked inside a concrete box without windows is a total hell for somebody like us, who are used to playing with our human pack on the beach every day. I wonder how those rescued dogs feel being locked away over a long time in a dog shelter. Don't humans understand that the most important for us dogs is to belong to our pack, run together with our humans when they do, and that being locked away in prison is very traumatic? The emotional suffering is unbearable. Not the food; it is the love that we need the most. Look at the dogs of poor people! Dogs still stay and love their humans even when they are poor, and their food is scarce.

Instead of feeling sympathy for our suffering, Vera and Diego got annoyed with us when Gogi and I, in protest, refused the food they brought us.

"'*No sean los jamoneros, malcreados*' (don't be spoiled touchy-feeling boys)," said Diego. "Maybe you were adopted by the foreigners, but you are still Cubans. There is nothing as important for Cubans as food; that is because food in Cuba is disappearing more and more each year. Since the Soviets stopped maintaining us, no medicine or goods are available in stores for the Cuban population. The fault is only yours, Benz. Why did you bark at our new Cuban boss? Why are you now refusing the food I brought to you? Protesting against being locked out? We keep you here because we have to protect your lives from Zoonosis; you are acting silly."

"What are you looking at?" added Vera. "Your food consists of leftovers from the meals of well-fed foreigners. You are very privileged and know nothing about the food situation for us common people in Cuba. Let me tell you while we are here, the thick walls of this bunker protect us from eavesdropping. I have to take it out of my chest. That little jar of Peanut Pan butter, brought by Frank, you stole last week from the kitchen table before it was even open, costs in Cuba more than my monthly salary," she growled angrily. "You rascal would say that you didn't know, and you took it to play because of its small size."

She went on lecturing me again, "Let me tell you that after it disappeared, Frank told me that he bought this jar for me to try its taste because there is none in Cuba. After you stole it, he thought it was me or Diego who took it out of curiosity to find out what was so special about this peanut butter in the little jar. You buried it in a backyard ground, hoping that nobody will notice it was gone. When Diego discovered where you hit this jar, Frank apologized and said that dogs in his country also love peanut butter. What do you know about the lives of ordinary human Cubans? What do we love to eat and what we do eat?"

Her frustration suddenly found an outlet, "The ordinary Cubans love eating, but there is nothing, except some beans and rice, available in our stores for our Cuban pesos. Why would you ask? Cuba is blessed with nutritious, rich mineral soil and a sub-tropical climate. Cuba was the breadbasket of America before the revolution. Why, after the revolution, were Cuban farmers forbidden to grow their own crops and vegetables? Why, after the revolution, was our meat brought from Russia and the cattle from Canada? What happened to our fish and sea products? Are we not a Caribbean Island nation surrounded by rich, warm oceans? Why are our fishermen prohibited from providing the Cuban population with sea products, which they were traditionally used to catch at sea?

"Cubans love the beach and swimming, but ordinary Cubans are not allowed to use a good beach. You, the dogs of foreigners, are allowed to enjoy yourself on the beach, and you can eat when you are hungry. We, ordinary Cuban humans, can't buy the essentials to survive and must invent how '*a resolver*' (to buy it on the expensive black market). We, ordinary Cubans, can't repair the ruins of our crumbled housing because our government invests only in resorts and hotels for foreigners. You, rascals, don't appreciate your privileges. If somebody will denounce me to the Cuban authorities for hiding a dangerous dog, I will be punished and will lose my job as a consequence - all thanks to you, Benz."

My only hope was now resting on Diego, who used to defend me. He is guarded and soft-spoken, but this time he supported Vera, "You are right, Vera, your training in the national economy makes you wonder why blessed by nature, we can not feed ourselves. Still, if anyone denounces you for hiding Benz, you will lose your job with this foreign joint venture and be listed as unreliable. No Cuban state company would ever hire you with such a mark."

"Sure," she said. "I can tell you here because nobody can hear us that I am pissed off. It is not sufficient that my Cuban employer deducts nearly ninety percent from my salary the foreign partner is paying the Cuban state for my labor. Still, in addition, they deduct the useless union fees. And that is not all; the crumbs they pay me as my salary is in Cuban pesos instead of hard currency. These Cuban pesos are devalued. Additionally, we are subjected to periodic debriefing and harassment by security.

"Nor I can take Benz with me to hide him at my home, for I don't have a home or apartment of my own. The building where I had my apartment in old Havana collapsed from disrepair in Old Havana, and I have to live in a very small room in the apartment of my married daughter. I lost my hope to have one day my own place," she added.

"Same here. The truth is," said Diego grimly, "that our only valuable benefits of working for a joint venture with foreigners are our service tips given to us under the table in secret by the foreigners. All foreign companies in Cuba are regularly helping their Cuban employees who otherwise would have no incentive to work. It is such hypocrisy. Everyone in Cuba is aware of these under-the-table payments, but everyone goes along with it as long as it is convenient. Those who are giving or accepting tips are breaking Cuban law and are risking fifteen years in prison under corruption charges for both parties: Cubans and foreigners. I only mention this to you, inside the concrete walls of this bunker, where nobody can overhear us; otherwise, we could get charged just for talking like that. You know this, right?"

"Yes, Diego, sometimes, my rage takes over me, but I do my best to control it. Don't worry, nobody could hear us in this bunker. In a moment, I will regain control over myself because I understand that the foreigners can not adopt me, as they did with these dogs, and I have nowhere to go to survive. I was trained and conditioned from birth to obey the orders of revolution. Now I am used to this condition, like the rest of ordinary Cubans, to live in this false existence, permanently hiding my resentments. It became my normal state. You, Diego neither have a choice nor must agree with anything our government wants, or you too will risk losing your means of survival."

"'*Ya nos metemos muela* (we already said more than we should have). *Así que dejan de ser majaderos los chicos'* (stop being the spoiled boys). We all are risking and suffering for you," added Diego, and with this, they left us alone in the bunker for the rest of the day.

All of our Cuban scientists and techs are also scared of 'meter muela', I thought. It looks like the ordinary Cubans are a pretty scared bunch. Probably they are hiding from Zoonosis as well. There must be a Zoonosis for Cuban stray humans. Is Colonel Beltran working with Zoonosis for Humans? What would happen if one day not only stray dogs but also stray humans rebel against Zoonosis?

We felt ashamed and ate our food, feeling guilty, miserable, and very bored. When Diego came to release us at night, Mommy Dora and Daddy Frank said, "We have the good news. No need to keep dogs locked all day in the bunker because we arranged for "ore-search" training of Benz according to their promised made to Comandante Tainted."

Basically, they arranged for Diego and me to spend up to six weeks at his cousin's farm to train me as an ore-search dog. Diego should be qualified to train me because he witnessed the work of Russian military mine-search dogs in Angola, where he served with the Cuban Army. Gogi will get a break as well. He will be allowed to stay at the house with our human pack because he was not denounced as a dangerous dog to Zoonosis, only I was.

Chapter 5

Early the next morning, Diego and I left for the farm that belongs to Jose - Diego's cousin in Santa Clara to start my training as an Ore-Search dog. I cannot help to brag about accomplishing this training with flying colors. It commenced with learning to relate to farm animals. You see, our Doberman breed was created to guard and not to attack other creatures, so it is naturally in my nature to be friendly with everyone on their territory – their house, not in my house, where I must protect my pack from the invasion of vicious creatures, whoever they are. So, I immediately became the happy friend of farm animals and the loyal protector of Jose, the farmer, and Diego's cousin, especially keeping in mind that the alternative was being locked in the bunker.

Jose, a young Gallego (the name for the people of Spanish origin in Cuba), a happy-natured, blond fellow with a fair but dark-tanned complexion, looks a lot like Diego but smells of his farm animals, wears rubber boots and a large straw hat. I learned that he is actually a young agricultural scientist who lives with his wife Mira – a skinny and sweet young provincial *mulata* smelling of milk and food cooking together with their 11-year-old son Pedrito in a small two-room hut. They are simple, nice but poor people who fed us well. I overheard that my adoptive parents paid them for our accommodations and food unofficially.

If I understood correctly from their discussions with Diego, Jose participated in a state experiment with independent farming co-ops. After the revolution, all land in

Cuba was nationalized and was used for large-scale industrial sugar cane production; however, when in the 90th the Soviet Union stopped supporting it, Cuba experienced massive famine across the island '*Periodo Especial*' (Special Period). The Cuban government was forced to reform its agricultural production. To that end, they allowed the creation of Independent Co-ops. Jose was a member of such a Co-op. These Co-ops were leasing the land from the state farm and working it.

"So far," said Jose, "it has not produced a sustainable income for farmers because they had to sell 80% of their product back to the state at the fixed low price. Previously fertile land they were leasing was ruined during decades of planting sugar cane for the Soviet market. To produce traditionally grown Cuban crops and vegetables, such as cassava, yuca, rice, potatoes, malanga, beans, tomatoes, carrots, melons, onions, and salads, Cuban farmers needed to fertilize the soil depleted by sugar cane and use the agricultural machinery. Neither fertilizers nor machinery was available at any price.

The farmers were allowed to sell the products of their animal husbandry on public markets because it is a criminal offense in Cuba (punishable by 15 years in prison) to kill their own cow." After a few drinks of '*aguardiente*' (alcoholic beverage), Jose complained in secret, "The only successful entrepreneurs in Cuba today are the criminal syndicates dedicated to stilling the life stock from farmers, if not for illegal meat resell than for demand of ransom from a farmer."

This is why Diego's cousin is grateful for my help to guard his livestock. His own dog Perro is too old.

"Cuban farmers," he said," have the land as usufruct, without property titles. They are regulated by an agricultural system that monopolizes production and distribution. They are overwhelmed with taxes, harassed with endless inspections, and subject to confiscation of their harvests and their farming equipment."

Pedrito - Diego's little cousin-nephew loved to play with me and my ball. He preferred to hang around us most of the time. Perro, their older cow dog, is submissive in character, so I didn't even have to teach him a lesson. He respected my space and my dominance, for he was interested only in watching cows, and my help was welcome. Neither has he shown any interest in interacting with me. Quite the opposite, he went hiding in the far end of the barn after we would finally retire. Diego and I also slept in a barn. It was pretty rough compared to my parent's bed, but I put up with it, for I loved Diego and our spirits were high. We were free to play and learn search techniques in the field, and once I learn them, I will become important, able to amuse my human pack, and with good luck, I might be able to help us all to get rid of Zoonosis.

During the daytime, Jose and Mira were opening the field with their ox. Pedrito and Perro were herding the livestock, and I helped them while Diego was digging in a forest and the fields to hide from me the small aluminum cans with some bits of sulfide and pyrite ore, given to him in Havana by our geologist from his collection. My job was to detect those hidden cans, including those which were hidden a few days and even weeks ago. I had to locate them not only in the daytime but also at night.

Initially, I missed some, but after a couple of weeks of repeating these tests, I was able to find them easily every single time. Diego rewarded me with the meaty bone every time I found them. He made a lot of fuss about my ingenuity and bragged about my success to Mommy Dora on a satellite mobile phone, which mommy gave him to take with us because the farm had no phone. He is very generous in praising me for finding aluminum cans with ore and stopped worrying about spoiling me as he used to do before.

For this, I love Diego. At night while humans eat and drink *'aguardiente'*, I accompanied their ox, two cows, pigs, and chickens for a good night's sleep at the barn. They obeyed me, and the farmer was happy because he said that Perro has slowed down quite a bit from old age. All was wonderful, but I was badly missing my home, my adoptive parents, Vera, and Gogi. I also knew that life with Diego on the farm was only temporal, and I was afraid that while we are playing games on the farm, the mad colonel might come again to hurt my pack. Despite having a good time on the farm, I felt that my duty was to protect my permanent pack, and I missed them.

Seeing me sad, Mira gives me an extra juicy bone or a bowl of my favorite *Arroz con Pollo*, which she cooks over a low fire behind the house in a really large skillet with a cover. She dredges large chicken pieces in the flour mixture with spices and puts them in the pan to stir until the chicken has browned. Then she removes it from the pan, adds the rice to brown it in the same pan, and adds the onion and garlic. Normally, I don't like onion and garlic, except being fried; they taste different. She fries the onion with garlic and rice mixture, stirring frequently, and places the chicken pieces, skin-side up, on top of the rice. In a separate bowl, she mixes the stock, and tomato and brings it to a simmer on low heat until the rice and chicken are done. I get my portion of this food for angels after she fluffs the rice with a fork and sprinkles it with some peas before she adds salt and paper. Mira is always right - it helps with the nostalgia.

Approximately one month later, more, or less, Diego announced that we were returning home. Mommy called us because we had to get ready for the visit of my possible savior – a special envoy from the Vatican. Diego explained that mommy and daddy believed that if I would help the envoy to find the treasure, the false accusations of a dangerous dog might be removed from me. Such a heroic deed might convert me into a dog important for the economy of Cuba, and the status of our Joint Venture would gain an important protector in the person of Fidel

Castro himself. Jose, the farmer, and his family will miss us; I know we too will miss them, but I was happy to return with my permanent pack.

On our arrival home in Tarara, I couldn't control my jumping provoked by happy emotions when greeting my pack. I was also anxious to show my superb new skills in search of gold. It was obvious that my human parents also terribly missed me. They couldn't stop hugging me, and Vera even dropped a few tears of joy while our pack members surrounded me with adulation. Gogi sniffed me for a long time, hoping to learn of all my recent adventures on the farm. He went sticking his snout everywhere into my body until I got angry and groveled at him, "No, bro, there were no female dogs on the farm. Let me better show you all those new tricks in ore-search I learned on the farm. I will teach you later, bro, but I am crazy missing the beach for now. Let's run to the beach," I suggested in my excitement forgetting about Zoonosis.

No luck, instead of the beach, Vera took me by the collar and dragged me away to the backyard, where she proceeded to give me a horribly stinking bath with disgusting perfumed shampoo. I didn't like it, but Vera was convinced that I still smelled of farm animals. After this special grooming, all humans admired my new looks. Finally, Diego and I gave them a brief demonstration of a smart ore-search dog I was, and everyone became convinced that I deserved, if not a Ph.D. in treasure search, then at least a very substantial piece of sausage. I graciously accepted the sausage and the admiration of the crowd, and, as it always happens, Gogi also benefited from a similar sausage, and this exhilarated me even more. I felt as if I had grown at least a few inches taller, and when the prestigious Vatican visitor came the next day, I was emotionally ready to steal his heart.

That morning, all our pack members, except my family, were given time off to allow me and my parents to meet our special visitor in private. Only Mommy Dora, Daddy Frank,

Diego, Gogi, and I stayed home to receive the envoy. Gaspar – the assistant of Comandante Tainted, came to visit us with a young, tall, slim, and handsome Italian by the name of Giovanni, who was polite, though a bit shy. Gaspar introduced him to us as an envoy from the Vatican and nephew of the Cardinal Secretary of State of The Holy See.

I politely sniffed his shoes and pants, he smelled of good disposition, and I sat down by him on my hind paws in the position of a good dog, then I appropriately switched my sniffing to the shoes and pants of Gaspar because I did not want him to feel ignored.

Gaspar is a middle-aged Cuban security officer. He was dressed in civilian, short, and lean, with penetrating dark eyes, good looking but smelling of tobacco, and with a stern and confident personality - a bit too domineering and businesslike (for my taste). His opinion will be an important factor in producing a positive impression on his foreign companion.

After the initial pleasantries and nice cool drinks, we all went upstairs into the office, where we felt more privacy. Giovanni explained the importance of his uncle, the Cardinal Secretary of State of The Holy See - a Prime Minister of the Vatican, who is the second man in the Vatican after Pope John Paul II. The Cardinal was in charge of representing the Vatican to foreign governments. When he received the inquiry from Fidel Castro about the availability of documentation related to the lost treasures of the Cathedral of San Ildefonso of Merida, the Cardinal asked Giovanni, his more adventurous younger nephew, to conduct the follow-up research.

Apparently, these documents, including the sketches of a map, were brought in 1898 by the priest Fray Rios of the Church of Nueva Filipina when he abandoned the Church on the arrival of soldiers of General Maceo who converted this Church into barracks during the War for Independence. He escaped with the documents on mules over the mountains to the village of Luis Lazo and from there to Havana, where the Arzobispo of Havana kept them in safekeeping for the Vatican. After the end of the War of Independence, the Vatican sent its envoy to Cuba with the mission to recover the treasures from the cave of Guanahacabibes. To this end, the Catholic Church purchased a large coastal area, but apparently, the treasure was not found, and the envoy returned to the Vatican with the documents.

At the beginning of the Cuban revolution, the Catholic bishops united in condemning the Communist Party that was governing the country because the revolutionary regime was promoting atheism, thus coming into direct conflict with the church. The Catholic Church became actually persecuted: the churches and the religious schools were closed, and the priests were exiled or assigned to re-education camps where they were punished by very hard labor in agriculture in awful conditions, starved, and without pay.

Now Fidel Castro was asking the Vatican to assist him in locating this treasure. To the Cardinal, it rang a bell. John Paul II's first pastoral pilgrimage to Poland in 1979 is rightly regarded as one of the key turning points of the Cold War because it ignited the revolution of conscience that made possible the Polish Revolution of 1989 in its unique form. The Cardinal thought that if Fidel Castro was interested in documents and maps related to the lost treasure of the Cathedral of San Ildefonso of Merida, it might be possible to negotiate the re-opening of communist Cuba to the Catholic Religion. So, he came up with the idea that the Vatican could help Fidel Castro in locating these treasures in exchange for the invitation of Fidel Castro for Pope John Paul II to visit Cuba.

Such a visit would largely help to re-open Cuba for the Catholic Church. Additionally, the Vatican would be willing to reward Cuba financially for the safe recovery and return of its valuables. They agreed on the amount of reward, and the Cardinal commissioned Giovanni to assist our friend Comandante Tainted in his efforts to find the treasures of the Cathedral of San Ildefonso of Merida. This is how Giovanni was sent by his uncle, the Cardinal, to work with Comandante Tainted in Cuba to organize the expedition and the team of local guides and speleologists of confidence. Geovanni was asked to investigate the use of the latest technology in metal detection to find the gold and silver stored inside the caves of Guanahabibes, while Fidel Castro will prepare his country for the forthcoming visit of Pope John Paul II.

At this point in the story Giovanni, like the salesman in English TV commercials, changed his mood and appearance. He looked intensely at Dora and Frank and inquired with a convincing smile, "I heart that you have in your possession the latest model of the magnetometer. You see, the large cave networks are too dangerous and often not easily accessible. The modern metal detectors don't have the sufficient power required to find different metals in different soil conditions as we are expecting.

We believe the powerful magnetometer might be more helpful in locating gold and silver objects by using a magnetic field of magnetometer at a significant distance and in a broad swath, changing its power on a fly corresponding to rock and soil conditions."

"Very sorry to disappoint you, Giovanni," Mommy Dora said. "I explained to Comandante Tainted that gold has no magnetic properties and silver has very weak; therefore, their electric response is simply too weak. For your job will be necessary to design and build a special high-frequency powerful metal detector. Our deep-water marine magnetometer can only detect ferrous metals; it is effective only for metal debris on the ocean floor, it must be towed behind the ship to find the magnetic signature of ferrous metals on the ocean floor, but it will not detect gold and silver hidden in caves. I already explained this to Comandante Tainted."

"Some of our cave networks have underground freshwater rivers, streams, and lakes draining into the ocean and ocean waters brought by the high tides and submerging the porous limestone. The mixed fluvial and ocean waters were collected for many millions of years from the surrounding valleys, draining them into the deep geological faults of the peninsula. They created these coastal caves and their networks. I thought that we could try to use your magnetometer in lakes and underground rivers inside the caves," argued Gaspar.

"The lakes, rivers, and streams are not deep and long enough to tow our magnetometer behind the boat. The minimum depth for our magnetometer is 350 meters. This is how it was designed, built, and calibrated. Still, apart from the issue of water depth, our magnetometer is not designed to detect the magnetic signature of gold, copper, and silver, for they are void of magnetism," insisted Dora.

"I suspect," said Geovanni, "that you might have another reason for refusing to use your magnetometer in our project. I am authorized by my uncle to purchase everything necessary for this job, regardless of price. I am prepared to buy it at any reasonable price which you will name."

"Yes, Geovanni, you are right; another reason is that some components of this magnetometer contain a small quantity of cesium - a radioactive isotope fission product of uranium-235. We are allowed to use it to detect the variations in the magnetic field of the underlying deep-sea floor as a part of our operation, but we can't sell it in Cuba. We suspect it could be regarded as a double-use technology. But honestly, all this is beside the point. The main problem is the absence of magnetic properties in golden, copper, and silver objects."

"Truly, this is very disappointing," mumbled disgruntled Giovanni.

Suddenly Gaspar stood up and pointed at me, "Benz is the ore-sniffing search dog, about whom Comandante

Tainted spoke as possibly useful in searching for gold and silver inside the caverns.

The attention of everyone now was turned to me. Dora made me a signal to bow. I got up and lowered my front paws, my ears lowered down, and my tail under my paws in a bow, just like Mommy Dora taught me. Giovanni was looking at me with sincere interest. "What a handsome fellow! How old is he?"

"His name is Benz, and he is a one-year-old Dobermann trained as an ore-search dog. If you are looking for an atomic detector – it is his snout. He can find anything you ask, gold and silver including, or any other object if he sniffs the scent of it beforehand. He is completely versatile and extremely smart. He was taught many commands in Spanish and English, and he knows nearly a thousand words. He can also dance or dive. Benz dance!" ordered Mommy Dora and made a circular movement of the hand over my head, which means a command to spin around in a small area. I was only too happy to be the center of attention and spun around several times until she stopped me.

Mommy Dora took off her earring and gave one to Giovanni and Gaspar, "Could you please bury this earring in the backyard?" she asked. "Take this trowel, please." They went to the backyard to bury it underground. When Giovanni and Gaspar returned, everyone, me included, went outside into the backyard, and Mommy Dora gave me to smell the scent of her other earring. Then Diego commanded, "Find!" I obliged him immediately, same as before during our training: fast and furious! I know too well the reward for my efficacy will be a delicious morsel of meat. Apart from that, it was an excellent opportunity to show the new trick I learned on the farm: to sit on my hind paws beside the location of my find and howl.

Indeed, I must admit I enjoy all this public attention and appreciation of my talents. Everyone applauded as soon as

I accomplished my performance, immediately locating and declaring my find of Dora's earring. I got a juicy piece of fresh uncooked chicken (I like that the most) as a reward. Mommy Dora repeated the same praise she made before in front of Comandante Tainted, about the dogs with the long snout, like me, can smell a million times better than the humans.

"Benz will also locate the nasty sneaks and spiders inside the caverns," proudly added practical Gaspar, repeating the remarks made by Comandante Tainted during my previous demonstration to him.

To prove the point that I was entirely in agreement with my humans, I rose on my hind legs in front of Gaspar and performed obedience to him. I liked Giovanni and wanted him to hire me into his pack to search the caverns. That should be a great adventure, a lot of fun, especially compared with the prison in a bunker of Carlos Prío Socarrás, and it will please my family. Most importantly, if I succeed, our human and canine pack might get rid of mad Colonel Beltran.

"Well, if you are looking for an atomic detector inside the cavern – you will not find anything safer than the snout of Benz," concluded Daddy Frank.

"I hope, since Diego was the one who trained Benz, you will hire him as a handler. We don't want to burden you with the care of the dog. We will be happy to wait for their return home when you decide that the task is accomplished," said Mommy Dora.

Chapter 6

My introduction to the hard plastic crate in the trunk of a station wagon driven by Gaspar was traumatic. I am not used to traveling imprisoned in a cage and obeyed only temporarily to pick up the Italian sausage-smelling garlic inside the crate. I am a dog and hate the smell of garlic, but humans are ignorant of canine needs, and, to tell you the truth, they don't really care to know. As soon as I went for the sausage, they shut the door of the cage behind me, locking me in this stupid, hard box - too small for me to stand and stretch out. I protested with loud barking, demanding my immediate release, but Diego asked me to calm down.

"This crate will protect you while traveling in a car; you will travel in it for your own safety," explained Diego to me, but I disagreed and refused to listen. I hated this plastic prison; it is worst than the bunker of Carlos Prío Socarrás. I lay on the plastic floor of this hideous box and desperately whimpered, looking through a little wired window at my adoptive parents, and of course, I won! They could not resist my suffering and intervened in my defense.

"No, he is not used to traveling restrained, and this box is too small. Benz is a large boy. It will be too dangerous for him to travel in this crate on Cuban roads: too many creasy drivers and large potholes on the road. If your car has an accident, Benz will be defenselessly locked in the plastic crate, too fragile to protect him. He will be better off with Diego in the back seat. He is used to traveling like that with us; it is safer and less dangerous for him."

Giovanni agreed, and I was let out from this stupid plastic cage and went to supervise Diego packing up our stuff, including my toys and plate. I also went to say goodbye to my younger blond half-brother puppy – Gogi, who was locked on this occasion in our parent's bedroom; its door I know how to open from the outside. I shared with him my excitement about forthcoming adventures in caves. I told him that I would be missing him and even tried to convince him that if the two of us will start begging together to take him for the cave hunting as well, mommy's heart will not be able to resist. No such luck; Gogi was too anxious. He was jumping and spinning instead of winning with me in a quire of this request. Mommy Dora misunderstood us. I tried to explain with my eyes and tail that I was grateful and excited by the opportunity of "cave hunting" with Giovanni, but at the moment, I felt confused and insecure because I didn't know what was expected of me to become qualified as a servant of the Vatican.

"Can Gogi please also come with us? It will be easier together," I was begging. Mommy Dora felt sorry for me but undeterred, "I know what is expected from the search dog but not from the Vatican servant. I do know for sure that within the Catholic Church, clerical celibacy is mandated for all clergy. So, if you want to behave as a Church servant and not as a stupid dog, stay clear of lustful sins, to which Gogi is so inclined."

Then we went downstairs for a tearful farewell and mounted the station wagon of Gaspar. I felt a bit scared and sad to leave my house, my adoptive parents, and Gogi, but this was my unique opportunity to save my pack from Colonel Beltran. Clearly, the fact that Diego was still my handler, totally dedicated to my needs, helped me to calm down. I watched him promising mommy and daddy to look well after me. Our training experience in ore-sniffing search on the farm built a trusting relationship between us. Together we are already a duo pack, and I had a very good reason for wishing to be away from Tarara for a while. Zoonosis is still hunting for a dangerous dog Benz, and I absolutely hated the prison in the bunker of Carlos Prío Socarrás. It was important for all of us to do whatever it takes to get rid of Colonel Beltran. We left; I took the back seat with Diego in the station wagon of Gaspar after I licked the faces of my adoptive parents, Vera, and Gogi.

We were traveling on the highway towards the province of Pinar del Rio, where our speleological team was waiting for us when I started feeling a bit sleepy and nauseated. Still, the discussion about me taking place between Geovanni and Diego woke me up.

"Does Benz always get what he wants? Diego, where and how did you find such a handsome and smart Dobermann?" asked Giovanni.

"Dora rescued him last year in Cojimar," answered Diego.

Still feeling groggy, I drifted away in my memories about this most important event of my life. I was sent away for cropping my ears and docking my tail while being only a defenseless, six- or eight-week-old puppy of Cojimar. I didn't know how to count time yet, but I remembered it as if it would be yesterday.

It happened in the early afternoon in Cojimar in the rugged and dirty backyard of an old ogre who wanted to amputate my tail and crop off my ears.

"Yawr, Yawr, Yawr... I am so scared, Yawr, Yawr ... so hungry and lonely," I cried, pinned to the ground with a heavy metal corroded chain in a strange junkyard under the hot Cuban sun, thinking, *This is the end of my world. I will die from thirst, and nobody cares to help me.*

"My Mami! Where is my Mami? Yawr, Yawr, Yawr... Where are my siblings?"

My tummy hurts from hunger. Why did these big human monsters tear me away from Mami's beautiful warm

nipples? What did I do wrong to provoke such punishment?
"Yawr, Yawr, Yawr…"

My day started by tossing around with my siblings, the way we always do when people throw us into our puppy box, nothing more than that. Yes, maybe we were yelping loudly, but what else to expect from five two-month-old puppies who are separated from their only protection and food – their canine mother?

Isn't it cruel enough that they dragged away from us our beautiful, loving mother and chained her all day long under the hot Cuban sun on the rooftop of their house? When they let her come down to feed us, she said she was dying from heat and thirst on that roof - there is no shade. Of course, the humans often forget to leave her water, and she thought that she would soon die and join those other Cuban dogs in paradise, who died under the hot tropical sun, thanks to this cruel Cuban tradition of keeping dogs on flat rooftops of their houses. She was losing her mind and strength on that roof, but that exactly was what the cruel humans want when they shout, "Shut up bitch!"

"Yawr, Yawr, Yawr…" Now, these scoundrels kidnapped me too! Yes, they snatched me from our puppy box by my scruff and tossed me into an itchy grey-brownish sack. "Yawr, Yawr…" *What have they done to my other siblings?* I still could hear my siblings cry, but I couldn't see them from that sack - only the darkness.

"This one is a macho (male); he will cost you five bottles of '*Aguardiente de Caña*' or '*una Tabla*' (100 Cuban pesos)," the human monster said.

Why is he asking 100 pesos? Is he trying to sell me? Probably he thinks that I don't understand his language. He is wrong. My brain and my hearing are as good or better than his. His brain was wasted long ago by alcohol. Mine wasn't damaged yet, and it is not my fault that humans don't understand canine vocals and body language. My snout is my main sensor detector and controller. All smells and scents are stored there forever, and this human monster stinks awful of alcohol and tobacco. God help me!

The shaking of the wired basket of his bicycle was shredding my unprotected body, and I yelped in terror. *Anyway, what are we, the innocent puppies and our beautiful mother, guilty of being punished like that?*

It felt as if this torture lasted forever; finally, the sack with me was removed from the bicycle and given to another old ogre. Another old man was smelling even worse than the first. He received me with drunken grunge. A skinny, humpy old fellow, smelling of tobacco and alcohol with skin made of dirty clay, dressed in unkept attire and a farmer's hat, grabbed me by my hind legs and cared me in this fashion to his working shed. I was so terrified that I couldn't even argue, especially if you consider my position: with my head upside down, I even couldn't yelp. All my blood went into my head, causing me total confusion.

When finally, he dropped me on the earth floor of his shed, I attempted to appeal by displaying my total submission, "Yawr, Yawr, Yawr... Please, please return me to my Mami. My dinner is long overdue, and I need the teats of my Mami, or I will die from the pain in my tummy."

He ignored my plea and asked my kidnapper, "This pup is too young without his mother feeding him; he might die. Who is going to feed him, and how much will you pay for docking his tail and cropping his ears?"

"You can see, he is around eight weeks old, and I will pay for docking his tail and cropping his ears two bottles of '*Aguardiente de Caña*' (a bootleg, low-quality sugar cane rum). I will pick him up a day after you finish with him, and don't bother about his feeding because he will be in shock and pain from the amputation and will not eat today. Tomorrow, you will return him to me."

"'*No mejodes*,' (Don't fuck me), can't do for only two bottles. I will need at least four bottles to amputate his tail and ears. For when you want it to be done?"

"As soon as possible, I will give you three bottles."

"'*Tumba eso*' (knock it down). I need one bottle just to keep this dog quiet and sterilized. This pup is very skinny but of a very handsome dark chocolate color. You could easily sell him as a guard in Havana for dollars, *Compadre* (close friend)."

"I don't have one on me right now but will bring you later," said the kidnapper and left.

"Yawr, Yawr, Yawr... What do all these Aguardiente have to do with me? Take me home to my Mami!" I cried, seeing my kidnapper leaving me in the hands of an old ogre man. He started closing the shed, which, having no windows, was becoming dark. Initially, the ogre ignored my cries and just pushed me away with his boot - right in my tummy! He also promised to hit me harder if I will continue crying. His brutality only called for more despair. "Yawr, Yawr, Yawr…" I cried in my helpless efforts to avoid his boots. *What the hell does he want me for? What did he say he will do with me? Docking my tail, cropping my ears, what exactly that is? Will he return me to my Mami after that?*

Thinking of my Mami, I suddenly remembered the problem with her tail: she didn't have one. Instead, where her tail was supposed to be, there was a large scar, and she acted like she just gotten stung on her tail. When it hurts, she just runs and hides. The same realization struck me about her ears. She doesn't have these beautiful floppy ears like my siblings and me. Instead, she has two narrow strips of skin always standing up in a vertical position on her head, making her look dangerously aggressive. She hated it and complained a lot about her ears by nervously shaking her head. She acted as from neurotic pain.

Additionally, she is often frustrated with us because she can't communicate with us -her own babies - the way we dogs do in our dog language. Our language is not vocal. We communicate with sign language, where our ears and tails are our tongs. Only the position of her tail and her ears could tell us what she wants us to do and what we need to learn, but since her tail and ears were amputated, she could not communicate with other dogs and could not teach her puppies how to behave. Tail up, tail down, at the angle, or tackled between her hind legs, flag tense tail, flagging tail, or wagging tail –these are opposite signs with a very different meaning. The same with the dog's ears: their position and tension express a precise and very specific message. But after humans docked and cropped her, she became completely mute in dogs' terms - a disabled dog without any disability compensation plus with neurotic pain.

I don't understand why humans have done this to my dear mother and why they want to do this to me. Would they cut the tongs and the ears of their own babies when the babies are just a few weeks or months old? I really don't know because until now I met only old people, and they all had their ears and were talking a lot. Well... maybe those humans I met were the humans of a low breed, and somewhere else, there are others: a beautiful high breed of humans with ears and tongs cut off, but I haven't met one yet.

My own father, whom I never met, according to my Mami, was a very handsome, large pure-bred chocolate Dobermann. The owners of my mother pretended that they cared for her when they brought him to meet with her, but as soon as my Mami fell in love with him, they whisked him away and didn't allow her ever again to see him. They never allowed her to share with him her pride: us - their puppies. The human owners of my beautiful mother and handsome father were motivated not by love for my parents but by the money they would cash for us - their puppies. They believed the pay for me and my siblings would be greater if our tails are docked and ears cropped.

55

This is a stupid, cruel, false, absurd, and distorted old-fashionable myth, worse than the creation of Doctor Moreau! They believe it would make Dobermann dogs look fiercer than they naturally are. The clients who purchase such disabled pups must realize how cruel they are. They mutilated their pups only for the sake of their own false vanity and thoughtless stupidity, causing the life of suffering to these pups. These humans are incomprehensible savages!

The realization of what expected me sunk my spirits: it would be better to die fast and young: less torture than living in constant pain and abuse, but I was too young and wanted to live. I dropped to the ground of the shed and stopped crying, attempting instead to investigate the opportunities to escape from my prison as soon as the ogre leaves and closes the door. To my bad luck, the ogre hesitated.

Why is he stopping and looking at me with suspicion? Did he understand my intentions? I wondered.

"*'Verraco'* (Stupid)"- said the ogre. "I should not leave you here unchained, for you are now worth four bottles of rum. It would be better if I chain you first and wait for *Aguardiente* for your anesthesia and disinfection."

O... you bastard, you are not going to get me, I attempted to hide behind the tools of the shed, but he removed them. He grabbed me by the scruff, lifted me into the air, and threatened to beat the hell out of me if I don't obey him. With me in his hand, he searched for a chain behind the boxes with tools. The one he found was too large, rusty, and too heavy for me, but he used it in combination with the rope and tied it around my neck. Then he chained me outside to rusted metal debris laying on the ground of his backyard, which resembled a junkyard. After that, he left me alone.

Fucking ogre..., the chain was so short and heavy that it felt like being pinned to the ground. Desperate and helpless, so far away from my Mami, I couldn't hold it any longer and cried as high as I could with all my strength, "Anyone, please help me before this monster starts mutilating me! Yawr! Yawr! Yawr!"

Chapter 7

Finally, in my agony of begging for help, I noticed a petite-framed, slim, middle-aged, sun-tanned woman dressed in a khaki shirt and shorts approach the backyard fence from the street side. She was staring at me, undecided about what to do. Her face was worried. Her eyes were filled with compassion.

"Yawr, yawr, help, help, don't go, don't leave me here!" I begged her in desperation with all my strength. "You are my only hope; please save me from these butchers," I cried.

She saw my struggle and broke her indecision. The backyard fence was not high, permitting her to climb it over, and she came straight close to me. She smelled of the sea and not of rum or tobacco. She was small and not intimidating. The only human females I met before were my previous owners - two angry and always agitated middle-aged women with bloated faces. This stranger, who climbed the fence, moved with an air of confidence but didn't look anxious or hungry, ready to steal an unsecured object behind the fence. Her slim oval face, sunburned short haircut, intense-looking eyes, and a khaki shirt with shorts gave her an unusual Cuban woman appearance; maybe she was a foreigner. Looking at me with compassion, she picked me up in her hands, not by the scruff as the monsters do, but with her whole palm holding all of my body supported by her palms. I was so greatly relieved and happy that I almost peed myself, and consequently her palm, from the overflooding emotions, but luckily, I gained control of my functions as soon as she spoke.

"Who are you, my little hero," she said, "and why did somebody tie you like this in the middle of the day to this rusty metal under the hot sun, all alone? Where is your mom or your owner?" She spoke with compassion in a voice and a strong accent, which I understood although I heard it for the first time in my life.

"Yawr, Yawr, Yawr, take me, save me, run with me away from here fast, run...," I begged, my eyes desperately telling her that I would die if not for her.

She was my savior, and I will follow her forever if she takes me with her. To express my gratitude, I started licking and chewing her finger. It was safe, for I didn't yet have any teeth. Instead, she looked at the unkempt yard with a small shack at its back and called out, "Is anybody here, please?" The old ogre appeared at the door of the shack, very annoyed by her interference.

"'*Hola Señor., perdoname*' (Hello Mister, excuse me) '*por saltar su cerca*' (for climbing over your fence). This little pup was crying, and I don't see anyone taking care of him. Is he yours?" she said.

"He is not mine, *Compañera*; he was brought to me this morning by his owner to dock his tail and to crop his ears"- the ogre replied.

"What do you mean to dock his tail and crop his ears? How and where?"

"'*Aqui mismo*' (right here), *Compañera*"- he answered and showed with his hand in the direction of his tool shed. I will restrain him here and crop off his ears and tail. I will need to disinfect my scissors for this job. I could use some rum for that. Maybe you want to help this puppy by buying for me the bottle of rum to disinfect the scissors, the wounds, and to calm him down?"

"Rum to disinfect the scissors! Barbarous! Are you serious? Why his owner wants to do something so cruel and barbaric to this sweet puppy anyway?" – the foreign woman asked, instinctively holding me tight against her chest in a protective gesture.

"Because this is a Doberman puppy, *Compañera*, can't you see? Dobermann always has to be docked and cropped; otherwise, he will fetch no value when sold."

The woman appeared horrified by his answers. She held me even tighter.

"How could anyone, *'cojones'* (dammit), think of mutilating this little sweet puppy for the sake of profit?"- she asked.

"Yawr, Yawr, Yawr," I wailed, urging her with my eyes, "Please don't leave me with the auger ever again."

Finally, she acknowledged the need for swift, immediate action and launched my defense without any further rationale or justification. All she aimed for was to save me immediately and at any cost.

"I want to buy this puppy right now in his natural conditions – untouched and uncut. Can you contact the owner to ask how much he wants for his puppy? I will buy him now."

Cuban looked at her in surprise: "You want to buy the Doberman pup with his ears unclipped and his tail undocked? It is unheard of; all Dobermans should have it amputated. And this is my job? I haven't been paid for it yet."

Bastard, he wouldn't mutilate a stray dog, only a Doberman, I thought. *Why, why should I have such horrible bad luck to be born as a Doberman? Can I pretend that I am not a Doberman? Even being a cat would be better, anything but not a Doberman!*

"I will do what it will take to save this little creature from mutilation," now the woman was pleading with the ogre. "I will pay the owner and you, don't worry, just give me your price. Please, call the owner, and before that, could you please give this puppy a little water?"

"'*No sea enojada'* (don't be angry)," the ogre said, offended, "I already left him the water, but he knocked it down."

The ogre left to bring more water and called the owner from his shack while we waited outside. I anxiously drank my water. Only then did I realize how extremely thirsty I was, and my instincts told me that my kind savior would not abandon me.

"Fifty American dollars for the owner and fifteen American dollars for me if you have that much with you right now," said the ogre in an aggressive tone of voice when he returned. "I will not waste any more time talking about this pup if all you will do is promise to return with the money later. You will have to pay me now or forget the deal," he said.

What a scoundrel this ogre, I thought. Even being a little puppy, I knew from discussions with my previous owners. I overheard before that the four bottles of '*Aguardiente de baja calidad*' (low-quality bootleg sugar cane rum) cost only two dollars.

My savior checked her handbag, and yes, for my good luck, she had enough American dollars to satisfy the ogre. She counted the cash, paid the ogre for me, and asked to take off my chain. I clutched tightly to my savior's chest as we left together. We exited the horrible backyard to the street, this time through the fence gate, which the ogre unlocked for us.

I took the opportunity to lick her shirt in a show of my appreciation. Her maternal feelings took over, and she responded by petting me with emotion. We walked to the white Toyota van waiting for her on the side street. Its driver, a healthy-smelling, clean-dressed Cuban, a blond with a short haircut and big blue eyes, looking busy but kind, was surprised to see me with the lady when we approached her van. He asked her where I came from. She obviously didn't want to talk about that and dismissed him. She only said that I would be coming with them, but she needed to decide what she could do about her previously set meeting in Cojimar. They agreed that she would attend the meeting while I will stay with the driver in a van. She called the driver by the name Diego, and he called her by the name Dora.

Not bad after all, I thought. *My day started with nasty scoundrels, and it was ending with nice and kind people in a beautiful new van with an air conditioner and clean seats.*

I was truly amused to see for the first time in my life the interiors of a van. It even had an air conditioner – so cool. There were many seats, all clean and softly cushioned. The driver of the van did not appear threatening or nasty at all. Actually, you could say he was looking at me with compassion and was very polite to both of us: Dora and me. He spoke with a local accent, he must have been a Cuban, like me. *I better watch myself.*

While we drove to Dora's meeting, I calmed down, but when she put me on the seat beside her and exited the van, I became very anxious and started crying again. I was scared that she abandoned me when she left, and I peed on the seat in fear. Diego put me on the floor, wiped and disinfected the seat with a nasty-smelling chemical spray. He explained to me that he didn't blame me and that I don't need to tremble in fear. He petted me and offered *galleta* (crackers). I couldn't chew it, for I didn't have my teeth yet, but I felt better because his offer was friendly, and I stopped my yelping.

Finally, after what seemed to be an eternity, Dora returned to our van. It felt marvelous comfy, and secure when she picked me up and hugged me while petting me. I felt that she, too, was happy; even the abusive Cuban afternoon sun couldn't spoil her delight in saving me. No human ever petted and hugged me before. I felt completely relaxed and fell asleep from exhaustion on her chest while we were driving to a neighboring village, which I later learned is called Tarara.

She woke me when we arrived at their large house. It was my first time inside a house of humans, and I was completely overwhelmed by its size. It was built like a concrete bunker on top of the hill of the seashore with two upper stories and one underground. This wonderful house was one where many foreign and Cuban people came to visit, eat, work, and stay with us.

Tenderly holding me in her hands, Dora called at the door of the house, and Frank - Dora's husband, overacted seeing me when he opened the door for us. Tall, a bit grumpy, middle-aged foreign intellectual with tanned skin, a kind face, and dark soft curly hair, Frank smelled of a barbecued chicken he was preparing for dinner. His delicious smell and I liked him instantly. Normally, he rarely interfered in Dora's affairs, except this time. They had never before had a small puppy of their own, except on occasions when Dora fed strays from the beach, who later followed her. Those strays were mostly adults and were regarded as temporal visitors, for they were free to come and leave on their own. They were accustomed to a free dog gang wandering the beach area where tourists might give them some leftovers.

"What is that?"- Frank asked, looking at me unpleasantly surprised.

"This is our new dog, an undocked and uncropped Dobermann. Say 'hi' to him," answered Dora.

"A Doberman – a fascist dog, an assassin of Jews and Blacks! Are you out of your mind?" burst Frank.

Who is a fascist dog? I wondered, and what all that means? Assassin? Who, me? He must be out of his own mind. Why is such a nice-smelling man calling me by these

names? Who are the fascists? I even don't know who the
Jews or Blacks are. How can I prove to him that I am only a
Doberman puppy?*

But Dora was firm. "With my mind intact or without it, this
puppy stays with us because he has nowhere to go. This is
the end of the story. If we don't adopt him, the cruel, stupid
people are going to crop his ears and tail off because, in
their minds, it increases the value of Doberman. I don't
know which Dr. Frankenstein invented this procedure, but
while alive, I will not permit these fools to mutilate this
innocent puppy for their stupid vanity and greed. After all, in
the civilized world of today, dog cropping and docking are
illegal, right?"

"Not in Cuba, dear. Where did you get him from? Did you
fight with his owners?" Frank asked sarcastically.

"No, we are his owners now. I bought him for sixty-five
American dollars, probably only a fraction of how much
Doberman puppy will cost in our country. I don't know for
sure because never in my life, have I bought a dog before.
All dogs we adopted in my family before were strays who
came free of charge from the street."

"Great, except we always said that we don't want to buy
a dog, we don't want to reward the dog traffickers. Right,
dear?" sarcastically pointed out Frank. "There are always
plenty of stupid people willing to harm others for vanity and
greed. Human history is full of these stories: banded the
feet of little girls in China, and deformed heads of human
babies in the Andean countries. Why are you surprised by
the cropping and docking of dogs? Can we save all Cuban
dogs from cruel people? Are you forgetting that I must
shortly depart abroad, and you will be departing at sea?
This puppy can't stay with us. It is him or me…"

"We can't save all dogs, but we can save this dog,"
answered Dora in a firm voice. "He is staying with us, and if
it would become necessary, he will accompany me at sea. I
will sneak him onboard. If you insist that I make a choice -

you can start packing up already. It is not fair and wrong to ask me to choose. I have to do what is right and have nothing else to add. You are not in danger; this puppy is," Dora ended the conversation and went inside the house with me in her hands, searching in the kitchen for something resembling a milk bottle to feed me.

Yee..., she said it well. In her mind, all the cruel human history apart and all the philosophical arguments and excuses, she had no choice but to save me. For that, I will love and protect her forever.

She took me to the tab where she washed me with funny, nasty stinky, bobbly soapy water and then dried me with the towel to the kitchen with me in her arms, where she found and prepared a bottle of milk with a rubble nipple. It did not taste like the delicious warm milk of my mother. Actually, it tasted bad and smelled of rubber, but in my hunger, I accepted this rubble nipple into my mouth. Then after having my cow milk bottle for the first time in my life, I fall asleep. The next day I had some digestive complications until I got used to cow milk.

By the way, don't take that as a derogatory comment, I love Dora, but her milk bottle tastes like a car tire – terrible. You really have to be starved, the way I was, to drink this awful milk. Unfortunately, this cow milk bottle was my only option. For some time, I would still dream of my mother's beautiful nipples and my siblings. I knew that it would be better if I don't torture myself thinking of them, for none of us knew how to find them. I fell asleep in Dora's hands under soft, salty, and moist sea noise from the beach coast with sweet-sour feelings: sad about losing my canine family but happy about my new human parents, my new house, and my full tummy.

The spirit of an explorer awoke in me the very next morning when Dora picked me up from the basket beside her bed and took me outside into the backyard to meet the sun and bathe in the grass. It didn't take me long to investigate my new home. Let me tell you it is big, full of daylight and freezing temperatures. It has a big terrace, and its living room has full wall-height glass. I could see from the terrace a dazzling sun-drenched deep blue sea stretching to the horizon and hear the faint sounds of crashing waves and the cries of seagulls. The best of all is the smell of seaweed and the fresh sea breeze. I understood that from now on, the sea became my destiny, and I absolutely loved it.

The pine and palm trees around the house's backyard are full of small birds and crickets. They make a lot of noise, but I was not afraid of them even when the black ones called *totis* crowded on the terrace to investigate me. It only took me a few minutes to get used to them; after that, I chased them away. Actually, I discovered how fast and easy it is to adapt to the air conditioner: two huge metal monsters living on the wall of the first level, one large monster in the office, and small monsters on the wall of each bedroom of the second level, push the cold air (humans call them air-conditioners). I am not afraid of them because I knew straight away that these monsters were not alive and were controlled by humans.

My new house was spacious. We use it for our offices and residence for the foreign members of the family. Mommy Dora and Daddy Frank are the alfa couple of this Joint Venture in Deepwater Marine Surveys working in Cuban territorial waters. I became the only Cuban member of the pack who was converted from a Cuban nationality to a foreign one by my adoptive parents because, as I was told, only foreigners are allowed to live in the houses of Tarara. This is how disregarding the fact that I was born in Cojimar, I became a foreign member of IAE and gained my initial working title of dog-explorer in training. Of course, this immediately changed my status in Cuba. You can say that by kissing a frog, Dora converted me into Prince, and not just a Prince but also into a Holy Dog of Cuban Caribbean Deep.

Chapter 8

Our house is very appropriate for our needs, except a bossy female dog was already living in the house. Her name was Pretty, a little blond stray from the beach, who comes and goes when she is pleased. Daddy Frank calls her 'our Cuban Lady of the Night'. It is very hot, so we all hang out in our air-conditioned rooms, but she likes lying in the sun in the middle of the road, hoping to get run over by a car of tourists, to take them to court, like often Cuban kids do, claiming huge court-ordered insurance payoffs, and settle down on the beach for a leisurely life of sand and chicken bones.

Of course, you will tell me that I can't have a well-informed opinion because I was allowed inside the human home for the first time, but I will answer you that I am young but not a fool. I figured out something right because I heard that from many Cubans who came to visit us. They commented that my good luck was extraordinary. Not just because I was born as a dark chocolate Doberman, meaning the gentleman's dog, and not a stray mix like Pretty, but because I was adopted by the foreigners and became a family member and permanent resident in their 4-bedroom house with a huge terrace overlooking the coast. Unfortunately, this good luck often made me the object of envy and jealousy from others, but I shall talk about that later.

The beach is only one block down from our house, but I am not allowed to run freely in and out to the beach on my own, the way this stray Pretty does. Instead, I am expected to stay in a house that demonstrates my different social status. The surrounding pines and palms shadow the terrace but let the sea breeze cool the terrace and charge me with exuberant energy produced by the strong scent of pine and seaweeds. It feels fantastic; I just love it. The pine trees are crowded with *totis*; they sing non-stop, always happy feasting on numerous crickets, which should be eaten anyway because they form a noisy racket and spoil the music of waves and seagulls.

I enjoy dozing while I rest on the terrace. Still, and most of all, I like to observe other illegal human visitors rooming in Tarara, mysteriously leaking into Tarara's beach despite the militarized guards' station, whose job is to protect the entrance. I like watching them through our glassed wall panels in the living room. The crowd of such visitors consists mostly of teenage Cuban girls called *'luchadoras'* and the gangs of stray dogs streaming from the nearby villages and highway to the Santa Maria del Mar beach in the late mornings. Both groups hunt for foreign tourists from the nearby hotel MarAzul and beg them for scraps. I noticed that foreign tourists, mostly male, treat young girls and stray dogs quite differently. They turn their backs and walk away from dogs trying to get rid of them, but they welcome the girls before they retreat with these girls to the hotel MarAzul.

The girls and strays come in all colors, but their popularity with foreign tourists is strangely reversed. Tourists favor the blond dogs and the dark Cuban *'mulaticas'* girls. Nobody understands the reasons for such discrimination. For example, we Dobies love all our colors: isabella (light tanned), red, dark chocolate, blue, and black. We never discriminate against each other because of color, but the tourists do. Well, maybe because, as Mommy Dora says, we dogs are smarter and more perceptive than the tourists. Otherwise, only God knows where my color would fit, being a chocolate Dobie!

Returning to Pretty, I would never leave our house to join the dog gangs at the beach in her place. I prefer observing all these beach creatures from my air-conditioned living room from behind the glass. She could also do the same but no… She prefers the stray gangs on the beach instead of my company. It must be her vulgar taste; she lacks discrimination of higher bread. You would think she is hunting tourists because she is hungry, but I can attest she is fed at our home. She just can't help herself and tells me that she is there not for scraps but on the call of her dog gang, which she can't abandon. I witnessed her and her gang competing with *luchadoras* coming via the beach from the nearby towns in scavenging for the trash deposits at night.

"This is extremely dangerous and is strictly forbidden," Mommy Dora warned Pretty, but I continued observing her scavenging in secret despite the prohibition. When I scolded Pretty, she dismissed me, saying that the trash is absolutely irresistible, and if she does not get it, the local humans will. How boorish, I am, personally, also curious about trash, still, with the help of my human teachers, learned to control this philistine instinct.

Sorry, it is extremely easy to get distracted; allow me to continue my story. On the first day of my arrival, the other rooms in our house were initially inaccessible for my examination. Located on the second floor, they could be accessed only by the majestic spiral-wide marble staircase, which I learned to claim only after a few days of practicing. When I finally could examine each of the rooms on the second floor, I got the full picture. Mommy Dora and Daddy Frank occupied one room. I was invited to sleep in their room in my basket, but I prefer the family's bed as a reminder to everyone that I am their adoptive pup.

I started by sniffing the items in their room. It had a large bed and a large desk with many drawers and boxes. I checked the bed; it feels great—a good bed to sleep on with my new family. I also checked two other bedrooms for foreign techs, and one large common room converted into an office for people working with Mommy Dora and Daddy Frank. These rooms are less interesting. They contain only single beds and desks because the techs will come and go, like our stray dog Pretty, not like me, who will be staying with Mommy and Daddy forever. At least, that was what I overheard Mommy Dora saying about me.

Still, the most important and best-smelling room in our house is the kitchen. It is on the first level. This is where all delicious action takes place, where the fragrance of the food is the strongest, and, where Pretty gets her wonderful food scraps. Fresh fish, chicken, and even beef or pork are cooked on its stove. Sure, initially, the fire on the gas stove scared me good, and I hid away. But after a couple of days, I couldn't resist the aroma of cooked meat, chicken, or fish. The smell drove me crazy. All these wonderful, tempting smells are very confusing because I still didn't have my teeth and had to drink the cow milk from the rubber bottle. Very frustrating…

Just to remind you, dog food was not available in Cuban stores, so we dogs had to, thanks to God, learn to eat human food, which in Cuba is unduly spicy for dogs. Mommy attempted to feed me with a mix of rice and some ground meat or fish - the same leftovers from human food they feed Pretty with. She said that she could start changing my diet because she noticed how, just for fun, I attempted to steal some from Pretty. I wanted to investigate if it was edible, but Pretty growled at me with menace. Mommy spoke with me a lot about Pretty. She said that Pretty and the other stray dogs are as good and loyal as the pure breeds. They are healthier, smarter, and more grateful by nature than pure breeds, which are often inbred. She said that we must love Pretty despite her loose manners. Pretty is older than me; therefore, she has a higher hierarchy.

Mommy wants me to ignore bad and to learn good dog manners from Pretty. She said that I must look after her.

Easy said than done – Pretty pays no attention to me. She has yet to accept my needs and my presence. Mommy didn't know that I decided anyway not to bother with the meal of Pretty in the kitchen because I was planning to steal the meat scraps and bones she hid in a garden, probably for her gang.

This bossy stray Pretty assumes that she knows everything better and that she is number one, except I am aware of the fact that my birth privileges are superior. Otherwise, why does nobody bothers with docking Pretty's tail or cropping her ears, just like they attempted with mine? Who she thinks is deciding what I can and cannot do? My teeth will grow soon, and, as a superior bread, I will start managing dog food distribution in our house!

Sorry for complaining, but she really annoys me. For example, I love to skate on the polished marble floors of the hall on the first level floor. I don't have real skates, but I have very long slender legs and huge paws. All I must do is race from one end of our living room hall towards the opposite end leading to the open balcony terrace and stretch my paws; they would slide on these truly polished marble floors like on an ice rink. Totis, who are crowding the balcony, take the flight in a panic with a lot of noise. It serves them right! It is just so much fun! I could do that for hours, but Mommy Dora and Daddy Frank, after laughing at me a couple of times and noticing disapproval of Pretty, forbid me to continue. Maybe Pretty again complained about me because complaining about me is what she does.

I don't understand why Mommy Dora and Daddy Frank are so protective of this fat dog! They said that I couldn't jump over her or bump into her because she is expecting babies. This is completely incomprehensible. How and why should she expect any babies to come when I have already come, and I am still a little pup? We don't need any more babies in our house. Sure, I will do all my mommy and daddy say because I want so very badly to please them and live with them forever. I have to allow, if I must, this blondie stray Pretty to have her babies. Still, I don't understand how she got them and how many? Where will these babies stay, in our house?

The next morning after my arrival Mommy Dora and Daddy Frank took me to the beach, and it became our everyday tradition. The sea was calm, a pale blue, almost the color of the sky, with a broad purple belt on the horizon called Gulf Stream. There were a few little waves with crests of form, looking like seagulls in an inverted sky. Initially, I had difficulties walking on the fine white sand, especially because it was hot, and Mommy Dora had to carry me on her chest. Don't misunderstand me; I am not complaining. I like it on her chest because it gives me a sense of security. Everyone on the beach can see for themselves which dog is a really valuable breed: me riding on my mommy's chest or all those freely running strays.

Despite his initial nasty arguments, Daddy Frank became very attached to me, and in a few days, I was already firmly planted on the family bed, where my position is at his legs. I follow him everywhere because he is my Daddy, the male alfa in our pack, and Dora allows him to say so. Only Pretty is still trying to boss me around, but I told her from the start that in this house, my mommy is Dora and not Pretty, so she should cool off, please.

The house training was another matter. The doors of the toilets became closed for me to prevent me from drinking its water. The problem was that I couldn't figure out how to use it properly, and instead of using it as humans do, I regularly went to drink its water. I had to teach humans how to react really fast and open doors for me to the backyard immediately upon my asking if they didn't want to embarrass me with unwanted accidents. It took humans nearly a week to learn to understand my emergency signals.

The time flew very fast for me; it was just so much I had to learn in my new house with my new adoptive parents.

After the first long weekend with my new family, Diego brought our housekeeper Vera. The other members of our scientific pack also arrived. Three of them are European: Tony - a young Englishman and Mike with Jim - two older Canadians, who came to Cuba to work and stay with us in our vacant house bedrooms.

They will be training those young Cuban scientists who are still only graduate students and need to learn practical skills of deep ocean survey. The Cuban scientists are graduate students in mechanics, marine science, navigation, electronics, and software. Great, I wanted to mingle with them because they all adore me and compete among themselves in teaching me games and tricks. They wondered how to name me because Daddy Frank needs to take me to the local Cuban vet to issue my formal adoption papers and schedule my vaccinations.

After meeting with me, everyone praised my dark red chocolate fur shining in glory on light and my big green eyes, which according to them, brimming with energy, intelligence, and happiness. They were especially amused when after smelling and licking their hands and feet, I demonstrated my skills of sliding on marble floors of the hall and across the terrace.

Many people come and leave our house all the time. They speak many different languages, but one thing they all have in common – they all talk to me and play with me. I became the star, the center of our universe in Tarara. Now it became clear to me that what I always needed the most was this attention.

I never ignored someone and would always show my gratitude for their appreciation of my talents by dancing around them, spinning, jumping, and licking anywhere I can reach: their face, hands, or their feet.

Unfortunately, Mommy Dora prohibited me from doing this. Instead, she wants me to sit politely beside her, but I am too young to stay still, so I learned how to amuse the visitors with brief performances on the marble floor without disturbing the people who are always chatting in groups. True, I love showing off since I discovered that this makes everybody happy, including me. I won the hearts of the audience and became the darling of the day – an object of well-deserved adoration. Even Daddy Frank said that probably when I will grow up, I will become a politician. I am not so sure; almost all Cuban politicians I see on TV are military and very somber people with concrete faces. This is why I decided to avoid a military designation. I saw a documentary on TV describing the military dogs – they all were kept in small metal-caged jails and released only on the chain. Who on earth would want such lonely prison life!

Thinking of how to name me, Daddy Frank decided that my fur color reminds him of his beloved car, recently expropriated by the Cuban government: a dark-red-cholate Mercedes Benz 450SL. He suggested naming me in honor of this car, which Daddy naively shipped to Cuba. His car was in impeccable shape. He thought this deluxe classic 1977 Mercedes Benz 450SL with low mileage was an appropriate car for us in Havana because Havana is famous for parading old American classic cars.

Daddy inherited this Mercedes Benz 450SL collection model car in impeccable condition from an elderly relative when she deceased. Her husband bought this brand-new luxury car, and a few days later, he died without ever using it. His wife inherited this car but was afraid to drive it due to her failed sight. She kept it in her garage for almost 20 years as a memory of her late husband, as if it would be a memorabilia piece. Not realizing that in Cuba, private driving of a Mercedes Benz might be regarded as an intrusion into the privileges of Fidel Castro's whose motorcade exclusively consisted of Mercedes Benz cars, Daddy Frank planned to use this car while he was in Cuba, leaving it behind for our Cuban team after his departure, except this car had a totally different destiny.

Daddy said that two months following his arrival to Cuba, the Cuban customs officers appeared at our door in Tarara, exactly on the day the car manufacturing certificate counted twenty years. They expropriated it under the pretext that the new Cuban law came into force that very day and made using twenty-year-old cars in Cuba illegal. Daddy protested, arguing that Havana was full of very old cars in truly very bad conditions. All these old cars were still cruising Cuban streets today and will continue doing so for many years in the future. He asked if all those cars will also be removed from the Cuban streets? The customs officers looked confused and embarrassed when Daddy Frank asked this question but shortly regained the assertive posture and answered that it is too late to expropriate all other older cars from their owners in Cuba, except for this one.

Daddy Frank continued arguing that the new law was not yet in force when he brought his car to Cuba, but they were adamant: the law came into force today, and the manufacturing documents of this car confirmed that the car is 20 years old and that is all that matters. When daddy protested, saying that he would prefer to return his car to his homeland, they said it was too late to do that. His Mercedes Benz 450SL has already arrived with Daddy Frank two months ago, meaning it has been already imported to Cuba, and now they received orders from the Cuban state to expropriate it.

Later, when Daddy Frank discussed it with his Cuban friends in private, they secretly suggested, "More than likely, a special new Cuban law was legislated for this car on its arrival to Cuba. You see, Comandante en Jefe Fidel Castro travelers around the country in a caravan fleet of impeccably looking Mercedes Benz sedans. Mercedes Benz's cars are the exclusive privilege of Comandante en Jefe in this country, permitting no one else to compete with him in Cuba. When the customs office in Cuba receives an order to confiscate the assets, they don't ask how legal that is. Their only acceptable answer is *'Ordename*

Comandante' (Order me Comandante). To justify that, they can easily legislate anything they need or want."

A few weeks later, Mommy Dora had her own related experience during the last week's reception in the Canadian Embassy a week after the car expropriation. She was advised by a Cuban envoy to negotiate this unfortunate matter of their car expropriation with another famous Cuban celebrity Comandante NoPants. This nickname Mommy and daddy gave him after her interesting meeting with him. Comandante NoPants is an extremely powerful minister in Cuba, and the Cuban people are even scared to pronounce his name, the same as the name of Fidel Castro. Instead, they all say HE and stroke their invisible bears. Mommy Dora followed the advice and solicited to meet with Comandante NoPants to discuss the unfair decision of Cuban customs to confiscate their Mercedes Benz, which was brought to Cuba in impeccable condition two months before the new law came into force.

Comandante NoPants granted her an appointment at seven o'clock in the morning in his Miramar office. When she arrived the next morning at his office, he received her there alone, still in his pajamas. She was completely taken aback when he started a discussion about the car while he was changing from his pajamas into his military uniform in front of her, completely disregarding any social norms of respect for the opposite sex.

Mommy was shocked. When Comandante dropped his pajama pants to change into his military outfit, she thought he was trying to intimidate her, but instead of feeling charmed by his cute gesture, she felt shocked and humiliated. She gravely asked for his permission to wait outside, which she was granted, but their sedan Mercedes Benz was never returned. Daddy felt so upset that his beloved collectors' model of Mercedes Benz was forcibly confiscated that he removed the Mercedes hood emblem from the car and refused to surrender it.

"The hood emblem from Mercedes Benz will be waiting for you for when you will grow up big enough to carry it," Daddy Frank proudly told me. This is how it became my calling tag and was attached to my collar everywhere I went. But for now, Daddy Frank hid it away and declared himself satisfied in his retaliation because he believed that without its emblem, the prestigious value of the Mercedes Benz 450SL was lost.

Chapter 9

During my second month of stay with Mommy Dora and Daddy Frank, I became a true protagonist in a continuation of drama with Mercedes Benz when a slick-looking Cuban gentleman, impeccably dressed in a beige business suit, arrived at our door. He did not belong to our expedition team and smelled of garlic, which I detest. He carried a big briefcase and claimed to be a lawyer of Comandante NoPants. He spoke with Daddy Frank in the downstairs hall for half an hour, and I lingered between their legs to hear what it was about. I did not like the way this lawyer was threatening and growling at Daddy Frank, demanding the hood emblem of Mercedez Benz, which daddy promised to me.

So, I decided to intervene personally to defend my property. I must admit that maybe I came too close to the lawyer's feet when I lifted my hind leg and peed as high as I could, on his light beige pants and shoes. Everyone was shocked, embarrassed, and surprised, except me. They all shouted in horror. Still, in shock from my visibly deliberate act, Vera came running to wipe my pee off, and Daddy Frank grabbed me and, with apologies, carried me away to the backyard. Fortunately, this had to cut the lawyer's visit short, because as he said himself, he needed to try to remove my urine from his best new pants urgently.

Daddy Frank loved the way I scored with the lawyer of Comandante NoPants because, as he shared later with me, his main disappointment about the expropriation of Mercedes Benz was with the way it was done – a blatant robbery with no apologies! This is how I became a hero of daddy, and from that moment on, he permitted me the mischiefs that nobody else in the house was allowed to, not even Pretty or any other dog from her gang, who occasionally would drop down to visit us in pursuit of Pretty. Still, the expropriation of Mercedes Benz left daddy with a bad taste in his mouth, but my mommy decided this incident wasn't worth quitting their project in Cuba, in which they and their friends have already invested personally. Looking back, they should have been adverted that it was a good indicator of what would happen in the future.

My brilliant initiative with the lawyer of Comandante NoPants made Daddy Frank feel vindicated, and he became my unconditional loyal protector, even when I would deserve a true trashing. Growing up on the seashore in a resort community far from Havana's air and chemical pollution contributed to my very healthy appetite, and everyone, not only our pack but also the local veterinarian said that I was growing super-fast. Despite being only a few months old, I have already become bigger than many known Cuban adult Dobermans are.

Still, I have to admit that later I felt guilty because, unknowingly, when I peed the lawyer's light-beige pants and shoes, I caused the first report to Zoonosis about our IEA housing and hiding a dangerous dog instead of simply rude pisher, the way I actually was. Fernando - manager of Tarara, whom Zoonosis called to inquire about the reported dangerous Dobie, answered them that he knew me, that I was still only a three-month-old pup and couldn't possibly present the danger. His calming answer gave Zoonosis a good excuse to postpone their ambush on dogs in Tarara. They would rather avoid it because it would require filling their monster track with additional fuel to drive from the city of Havana to Tarara. They had their own alternative needs for that fuel and decided instead to place me on their list for monitoring as a possible future dangerous dog. Meanwhile, there was not a single dog in Tarara or Havana that would not stare at me with respect and envy when meeting me.

Especially after I became six-month-old and started wearing my emblem of Mercedes Benz when I proudly accompanied our exploration team everywhere, they went in Tarara.

Yes, you heard me well; my teammates later called me a seadog for working with scientists from all around the world on board our ship, where they trained the Cuban personnel in the science of deep ocean survey. But before I came on board of research vessel and went with my teammates at sea, I had to become an ore-search dog. It is not an exaggeration to say, I have become the first and the only Doberman ever involved in complex and exciting investigations of the coastal caverns and deep ocean waters of Guanahacabibes.

Sorry for getting ahead of myself again; for now, just permit me to return to my story of how I became a working dog but first, allow me to share with you a story about my learning of becoming a babysitter. The truth is my success as an explorer didn't repair my guilty feeling about my clumsiness with puppies and how it affected Pretty. She was becoming very lazy and fat. She stopped running with her gang and spent most of her time in the corner of our terrace. Her character changed from grouchy to paranoid. She was completely ignoring me and spent most of the time digging the ground in the backyard, and after that, she would obsessively lick her paws.

Frank contracted a local carpenter to build a fence in our backyard, which became converted into a dog pen with a large doghouse inside - her own doghouse inside her own pen in our backyard. I didn't take much interest in this doghouse because I was so very busy with my lessons in English and Spanish for obedience: sit, heel, down, wait, stay, come, off, up, run, over, through, steady, search, find, fetch, forward, chase, and worst of them all is the command 'drop'. It is not easy, but my numerous human teachers as well as special TV American channels for dogs, available only to us foreigners in Cuba, have helped.

First of all, I had to get used to my dog collar. The collar and my tags are all large and made of metal. I didn't like them at first, except for my Mercedes Benz emblem. Initially, it was embarrassing to walk on the leash. I was dragged around like a Prisoner! Then I noticed the effect of my dog collar with tugs and leash made on people, and especially on other dogs in Tarara when we walk on the streets, and I changed my mind. I noticed everybody's surprise, admiration, and spite when I walk on a leash in Tarara. They all: Cuban dogs and people would look at me with respect and envy, *"'Mira a este mangon imperialista! Este no jama los desperdicios como nosotros.'"* (Look at this Great imperial Mango! He doesn't eat from the trash the way we do.)

"'*Pa'l carajo*' (damn you) even the dogs of superior foreign beings are smelling of the sausage and cheese, we don't even remember how it tastes!"

Let me return to Pretty. Carpenter took many days to build a large doghouse and a large, fenced pen in the backyard. Pretty went into the backyard and occupied the doghouse when it was ready despite my warning not to rush into it. Sure enough, I was right -this doghouse was trouble because she cried from pain later at night for a long time. Mommy Dora and Daddy Frank spent that night in the backyard with Pretty, returning only after Pretty calmed down in the early morning. They said that Pretty had five healthy babies that night.

When finally, in the morning, daddy allowed me into the backyard to see her and the babies, I found Pretty curled inside the doghouse, clinching tight her babies between her thighs. All I wanted to do was to see them, but Pretty hid those little creatures, who looked like white and yellow rats, and she crawled at me so viciously that I knew she would kill me if I tried to come closer.

Initially, only Mommy Dora, Daddy Frank, Vera, and Diego were allowed to look after Pretty and her babies. I

81

was banned altogether, but later the next day, I sneaked in and observed Pretty feeding her babies at her nipples. When the people noticed me watching Pretty, they all growled at me, including Mommy Dora and Daddy Frank, and took me away inside the house. Mommy said to me that I must respect the wish of Pretty because she is the mother and has authority over her babies. If Pretty growls at me, she knows better what should be done. But I was pissed off: such discrimination! All pack members were allowed to see those babies, but not me!

Little by little, her babies were becoming quite cute, like little balls of fur, especially after their eyes have opened, and I was dying from curiosity in my desire to see them closer. Dora told me about the true reason behind Pretty being scared and nervous with the young. The children from Chernobyl, Ukraine, living in Tarara, stole from Pretty her first three beautiful babies born in our house the previous year. That happened before I was even born. Pretty originally came from the beach. Apparently, one early morning a year ago, Pretty picked up Mommy Dora and Daddy Frank on the beach of Tarara and followed them to their house, where they fed her.

Smart beach stray, after she knew where they lived, she started coming to their house every day and consequently became a permanent visitor. A few months later, she gave birth in their house to three gorgeous blond pups. One night, when the pups were nearly one month old, they vanished, and despite all efforts of Pretty, Mommy Dora, Vera, and Daddy Frank to find them, they were never found. The guards of Tarara said that they have seen the Chernobyl Ukrainian kids running with pups in their hands into their own housing, located not far away from ours.

The guards said these kids were seen before trying to sell the other stolen pups to buy alcohol in secret. Mommy Dora went to see a teacher of Chernobyl kids, but the teacher said he didn't know anything about the puppies. Mommy Dora asked the children themselves, and, of course, they too never admitted to stilling pups. But the puppies were gone, and Pretty was terribly grieving, and possibly she became suspicious of the young who approach her pups. Obviously, she included me in the group of those vicious vandals. This is why Pretty lacked respect for me.

All Mommy Dora could hope for the pups was that Chernobyl kids would probably sell them to more responsible adults. She willfully refused to think that children were capable of abusing the little one-month-old puppies, but Pretty continued grieving for her babies. She didn't finish feeding them. It was too early to remove her babies from their mother's milk. She felt desperate and became depressed; she wouldn't even eat her food. Mommy felt that Pretty was right to worry. This is why she contracted the carpenter to build a doghouse and a large, fenced pen in the backyard this time.

Then the unexpected happened. As soon as the second litter of pups became four weeks old, Pretty suddenly changed. She began allowing me to see and play with the pups, but she started abandoning them between their feeds only to disappear to the beach with her old gang, just as before. The pups already could see but still had no teeth and could not maintain a balance. Pretty would negligently leave them on their own between the feedings. On my questions about this change in her attitude, she said that she could not take it any longer. She didn't have enough milk for all five pups that grew large and desperate to soak more milk. She said that they were biting her too hard, and she needed to forget her frustration as a mother by escaping from her own desperation and guilt. The only way she knew how to do that was to run away with her old gang of strays.

Vera and Diego felt obliged to assume the often-unsuccessful task of feeding pups from the teaspoon and baby bottle, and I had to take charge of these pups the best I could, between their feedings. There were five of them:

some blond and some black and white; and they were running across the opposite sides of the pen. Then the tragedy happened. I was trying to pick the puppies up from the pen area with my teeth and bring them back into the doghouse. Still, I haven't learned sufficient control of my powerful jaws yet. My new rapidly grown teeth provoked a terrible accident: I didn't even notice how I broke the neck of one precious puppy, who acted stubbornly in his attempts to escape. The puppy cried in agony, and the hell broke. Puppies cried, and everybody shouted, accusing me of murder. I was completely terrified of myself.

Vera, who noticed what happened, removed me from the backyard and locked me in a bedroom; after that, she went to rescue the hurt puppy. Too late, it was dead. I never saw that poor puppy again, and when Pretty returned from the beach, she went looking for that pup without success. Dora, Vera, and Diego were very mad at me and even refused to talk with me for the rest of that day. I was terribly worried about the poor puppy, and only later learned from Frank that the puppy has died.

In comparison with others, Frank wasn't blaming me but was rather critical of Pretty, who continued, according to him, irresponsibly abandoning her babies. I was relieved that someone spared a little male solidarity for an involuntary assassin. Daddy demanded that Pretty gets her act together or he will immediately get rid of the rest of the babies by offering them for adoption to anyone, including Chernobyl children, but Pretty refused to stay put. An important foreign investor was arriving in Havana to meet with us in our office in Tarara, and Mommy Dora started frantically offering pups for adoption. Except for one - a blond male pup named Gogi, all puppies were adopted by our Cuban friends.

Once again, I was admitted into public life and even attempted to mend my relationship with Pretty and her son Gogi, who became my younger brother. Gogi was an interesting pup. He acted and looked like a little lion. By the way, nobody knew what his name really meant; when others asked about it, they were told it meant 'to go' in English, but I overheard in our bedroom a conversation between Mommy Dora and Daddy Frank about the name Gogi. In reality, it was the original Georgian name of ex-Soviet dictator Stalin. I guess the lion looks of this puppy and his independent but foolishly antagonistic character had something to do with his name, but they didn't want anybody to know its origins not to open the door for unfair interpretations. As soon as Gogi was housebroken, he assumed his baby position in a family at the feet of Mommy Dora. I became the older brother of Gogi, but in exchange for schooling him, I demanded some respect corresponding to my higher status in the family.

Pretty would continue visiting us at her pleasure. She would come to eat with us every day and then escape to the beach with her gang until Diego and Mommy Dora kidnapped her to take her to the local veterinarian for spaying. She returned from the veterinarian the next day feeling very sick and emotionally upset. She refused to tell us what happened to her at the veterinarian, but she obviously felt mistreated and didn't talk to me. I noted, though, that her tummy had stitches, and she was in pain.

As soon as she recuperated, she disappeared with her stray gang to the beach again. This time she even stopped coming to the house to eat, and little by little, she stopped coming into our house at all. She obviously could not forget the pain she experienced from her spaying operation, except for some rare occasions when she would join me and Gogi in our morning work at the beach. Gogi was in particular very happy to see her, but not even Gogi, Dora, Diego, or Daddy Frank, could understand her true reasons for refusing to visit us in our house again. I believe that the death of the baby was too hard on the mother, and Dora felt personally guilty for instead of respecting the wild nature of Pretty, she took her spaying.

"Probably I was wrong when I decided what is better for Pretty when I interfered with her wild nature," she said, "forcing her to stop motherhood against her will is an act of terror performed on a free dog. The operation of spaying her was extremely painful, and she took more than a month to recover from it. It was my fault; now Pretty lost her trust in our family. Terror might deliver obedience (thanks to a chain or fence) but will not produce collaboration because it is based on fear and not on trust. I shall learn this lesson and never again use force if I want to preserve trust, only by persuasion through love and education."

Mommy Dora is, I believe, partially correct. My case is different. I trust Mommy Dora and Daddy Frank because they saved me from abuse. I feel safe and proud to belong to my human pack, while poor Pretty lost her trust in the safety of our home and returned to her original stray pack of dogs on the beach. While some dogs and people are more afraid of freedom (since it entails a responsibility) than of terror, they are willing to trade their freedom for the security of food and a roof over their heads. It is just too sad, especially for Gogi, that Pretty didn't learn to trust humans. After being spayed, she lost her trust in our family and preserved it only for her pack of strays on the beach. Belonging to a particular group based on the original trust is probably the most important instinct that defines us all: dogs and humans.

Chapter 10

I learned to walk on a leash with my human pack everywhere in Tarara. We went to the stores, cafés, restaurants, and even gym clubs – all are only for foreign clientele. For curiosity's sake, and not because I like machines, I tried to use the treadmill tracks delivered to Tarara on a humanitarian US health assistance program.

"A round business for Cuban state but not for you, Benz. I am not paying the hard currency for your membership in Tarara's gym club," said Mommy Dora.

Stingy and discriminatory, I thought. *The American humanitarian aid paying for the gym's equipment while the Cuban people are starving? The Cuban government is using this equipment to sell gym services to foreigners for hard currency. What is it about the Cuban people or dogs? American humanitarian aid to Cuba is not paying to feed them but to exercise the foreigners? Very confusing...*

Tony, Mike, and Jim, also talk a lot with me while walking me on the beach and the streets of Tarara. They taught me to fetch a ball and swim in the warm coastal waters of Tarara. I learned that the deeper water towards the horizon is quite different. It is due to the Gulfstream surface current being strong and turbulent. We don't have to worry about the possible danger from sharks because, as my friends told me, the Cuban state fishing fleet exterminated most of them in the Cuban coastal waters by targeting them for their fins. They are sold only on foreign markets and for the local manufacturing of so-called Cuban biomedicine, probably because the locals don't trust its powers.

We usually come to the beach in the early morning when the people of Tarara are still asleep, and the beach is still clean with a cool breeze. The seagulls are hunting for food and occasionally compete between themselves; that is when I get to chase them into the water. Water is mainly clean in the morning but smelly of seaweeds with the small crabs hiding in the sand waiting for a tide to wash them back into the sea. I like digging them out. Blue *medusas,* known as blue bottle jellyfish or 'floating terror', are often bordering the shore, and I try to avoid them because they burn my snout a lot!

In the early morning, the beach is ours. We swim and play by chasing balls and seagulls. Later in the morning, the beach becomes invaded by young *'luchadoras'* and stray dogs from surrounding Cuban towns competing for the best positions on the beach from where they hunt for foreign tourists. They are mysteriously allowed everywhere and tolerated, despite the official prohibition.

Generally, our daily agenda is full. We awake early morning and jump on the floor from our family bed to fight over who gets to grab the sandals. If we find them unattended on the floor, we run with them to the kitchen where Mommy Dora and Daddy Frank are drinking their morning coffee before departing with us for a swim and seagulls' chase. On our return home from the beach, the other pack members will also get up. After the breakfast prepared by our Mommy Dora, Gogi and I usually take Tony, Mike, and Jim back to the beach. Again, we get to swim and chase seagulls, then show our skills to the public, especially to the pretty *'luchadoras',* who would start slowly crowding the beach. After that, we return home and join the rest of our team for their daily briefings and work planning.

My teachers bribe me with little bits of meat into learning new words and commands in English and Spanish. I even learned to read some words by associating the shapes and numbers of their letters with the specific items of my interest (food, water, toys, and so on), but I can count only to ten, thanks to learning the counting of my toes on the front paws.

The skill I cannot accomplish so far is writing with my paws. Instead, I sign all important places by peeing them as high as possible, so everyone will note how tall, large, and important I am.

I have a very strong sense of premonition about those humans or animals who have vile intentions towards my team or me. It rarely happens that someone would feel afraid of me, for I advertise my friendly disposition to all we meet, except those I can sense, thanks to my instinct, have serious vile intentions and/or are scared of me even before I meet them in person. I can't help but start growling five minutes before we even see them. This way, my human companions know beforehand when somebody unfriendly is about to appear in our view.

I think it is my wolf's nature and not my personal defect. Even when I meet the hopelessly scarred humans, I try to convince them to calm down, but most of the time, the scarred types misinterpret me and start hysterical shouting at me: "This dog will bite me, take him away! go away!" and so on... With those I just give up, they can't be helped. Our pack members tell everyone that there is no need to be afraid of me because I don't bite, but if you ask the lawyer of Comandante NoPants, he will tell you how I marked him with my pee and probably wasted his new pants forever.

Gogi also hangs around us all the time. He was vaccinated and officially adopted by my parents as an amber-colored mix. I teach him everything a respectful dog of Tarara needs to know. He learned to walk with us on a leash, and he can chase the seagulls on the beach, but he is not that smart about his place in the world. Just like Pretty, he likes to be free, and I have a very hard time explaining to him that our house is a working place, and we have to become working dogs. We are learning at least a couple of dozen of new dog commands every day, and we must communicate in English and Spanish.

I do my best in teaching Gogi, but he is so cheeky! I even told Gogi my true story about a scoundrel from the beach who tried to kidnap me when I ran free chasing the seagulls far away on the empty beach one early morning. The scoundrel grabbed me by my collar and tried to drag me away, but I barked loudly for my human pack, and when they didn't appear, I bit the scoundrel on his leg and attempted to run, but he was strangling me by my collar until I managed to turn around and knocked him down exposing his throat.

Luckily my humans arrived and took me away before I have drawn his blood. They said it was important because the police would never protect a dog in a struggle with a human. It should have taught Gogi a lesson. Definitely, freedom has its perils, and only the strong will survive, but you still might be in trouble unless you have your pack dedicated to protecting and supporting you. This is my lesson for today. If you got the right pack – cherish them, protect them, and they will protect you.

No, I don't have unrealistic expectations about Gogi. I know that he pays no attention to my lecturing. Good-looking smart-ass, he lacks the patience required for learning complicated human communications. I am not talking here about the Internet, and satellite data, which our human pack members are using every day to prepare for their forthcoming ocean expedition, but about some true social conscience.

I want him to become more than a 'lumpenproletariat' (in Marxist terminology, these are the lower orders of society not interested in revolutionary advancement) like his mother Pretty was. He should learn to understand all basic English and Spanish commands and even the basic use of computers to interpret my messages, which I will send him from the sea after we finally depart for our expeditions since he is planning to stay with Daddy Frank, Diego, and Vera to handle our office onshore.

To this end, we both attend the training workshops for the Cuban team, learning about their work and their commands for using different ocean survey equipment. Recently we heard about their troubles with Colonel Beltran, their new Cuban boss, a new mean man about whom I already experienced bad premonitions. Maybe this Colonel Beltran can also receive my telepathic message and will quit on realizing that I mean business in protecting our home. This might mean the end of our problems with our new military partner in Cuba. Let me explain what I know about this new Cuban partner.

The Cuban military decided to take over all foreign Joint Ventures (IEA) in the marine field. They could only accomplish such a takeover if the existing Cuban partners surrender their positions. Some Cuban partners have surrendered voluntarily, but others continued resisting.

Those who resisted were removed by force, leaving the foreigners in those Joint Ventures with no choice but to work with the Cuban military. The trouble was that the foreign companies felt that their Joint Venture contracts with the Cuban partners were unfairly breached. Our Cuban team members heard the rumor that Nelson, head of our Cuban civil partner, was forced to resign. He fled the island by scuba diving twelve nautical miles across the Florida Strait towards the Florida Keys, where he was picked up by somebody friendly.

If that is true, then what has happened to his German shepherd Guapo? Guapo did not learn to scuba dive. Was he abandoned on the beach? Did he join the gang of strays on a beach? We must find him straight away, I thought, *and adopt him. Guapo admired Nelson. We better help him with the trauma of losing his master.*

Everybody on our Cuban team was confused. I heard of their fears about having to work for their new navy boss Colonel Beltran. The foreign members of our pack also could not comprehend how it became possible to replace an existing Cuban partner with the new one without consulting and getting the formal consent of foreign partners. The foreigners working in Cuban Joint Ventures refused to believe it. It was the moment when I perceived the danger was clouding our horizon. Cuban Zoonosis for Humans is probably on a hunt!

Even before I met Colonel Beltran, I was getting really bad vibes about him. Everyone knows that I am always an overly social and friendly dog, friendly with all the visitors and passersby, but that day I felt different. When he came to our office for the first time, my nerves were shocked by the dangerous sensations at least ten minutes before his arrival. My ears and tail went up, and my legs became menacing stiff, and ready to jump.

Dora and Frank were absent, and it was Diego and me who opened our door for Colonel. The foul smell: combining really bad cigarettes, alcohol, and poor digestion, almost knocked me down. But worst of all are his vile, killer intentions of the assassin. The image of my best canine friend, the German shepherd Guapo, who was abandoned by Nelson after escaping from the Cuban military, came to my mind.

I felt that this man was the enemy of my human pack who is preparing a vicious attack to hurt us and probably steal all our food. I did my best to warn Colonel that I protect my pack with the traditional obvious physical assertion and loud, aggressive barking before lunging at him. He got my message straight away and left, closing the door behind him.

Diego dragged me away to the backyard, but the Colonel was afraid to enter and didn't want Diego to open the entrance door regardless of my being locked in a backyard.

When Colonel left in his car, and Diego returned with me to the house, he looked concerned despite my affirmations of being calm and sitting down in a position of "good dog" when listening to his chastising.

I was afraid that it wasn't the end, and the enemy might return. I was right; he has. A week later, he came back, again without warning. Everybody was present during this second visit, and our team was working in the office on the second floor. The feeling of danger came again over me nearly ten minutes before Colonel physically arrived in his car at our door. I started a combative warning bark; then I lunged at our main entrance doors of the house because I already warned him last week that I was on the job defending our house.

Surprised by my impertinent behavior, Mommy Dora attempted but not succeeded in calming me down. She didn't understand that my intuition alarmed me of the approaching enemy. Daddy Frank had to come to help her to drag me outside into the backyard. Still, I continued warning them of the enemy even from a backyard by jumping and aggressively barking my message: "Zoonosis for Humans is coming!" I don't know if they understood my warning, but it was such a loud show that my bark could be heard on the beach and attracted the attention of tourists and the management of Tarara.

Diego, known for being vigilant, said to Mommy Dora, "I believe that our new boss Colonel Beltran is on his way to our office. I watched Benz acting like this only once before. It happened a week ago when Colonel arrived to see you without the previous notice, and nobody else, except Benz and I, were present. You would not believe it, but just like today, Benz became very agitated even before Colonel Beltran arrived, and, for the first time in all his life with us, I observed Benz wanting to attack a person. The paradox is that this person is our new Cuban boss, who was scared away by the aggressive barking and lunging of Benz. I dragged Benz away and locked him in the backyard. It took me a while to calm Benz down before I returned to the front door – Colonel Beltran was already gone without even saying goodbye or leaving a message for you. Permit me to make a bet with you that he is on his way and is about to arrive here again."

"One bottle of rum will do?" asked Mommy Dora.

"'*De-acuerdo*'," agreed Diego.

Chapter 11

"What the eyes don't see, the heart doesn't feel. I know you told us Colonel Beltran had come about a week ago. We missed his surprise visit, but you forgot to mention the aggressive behavior of Benz. The only other occasion I know of Benz reacting aggressively to humans or animals was when a scoundrel attempted to steal him from the beach," recollected Dora.

"You are right. I also never before seen Benz acting aggressively towards our visitors. We, the Cuban employees, are all nervous about forthcoming changes in the work of IEA under a new military partner. This probably is the reason I haven't mentioned it before," said Diego. "Perhaps it was a canine's extrasensory perception that provoked the dog's reaction to the hostile intentions of Colonel."

"Nobody wants to speak about what is going on because they are all terrified by their new Cuban boss," grumbled Mommy Dora.

Like the rest of our human pack, Dora is still in shock from a recent takeover conducted in a brash military manner. Quite unfair and annoying, wouldn't you think?

"All foreign joint ventures in this field, I heard, had good relations with their previous Cuban partners but were told it was irrelevant; the military takeover was decided," said Diego.

"Yes, I heard that from our Cuban lawyer as well," said Daddy Frank. "He told us, 'You already invested into the joint venture IEA, unless you comply, all your investments will be lost. You could not recover them from the Cuban military if you decline to operate. I also doubt that they will allow you to remove your equipment from Cuba. Most likely they will confiscate it claiming damage by your breach of contract.'"

What investments is he talking about? I wondered. What equipment are they going to steal? I will not allow that.

This is why when, without previous warning, Colonel Beltran arrived at our office in Tarara for the second time, I had to attack him. As the proud and honest guard would, I declared that I protected our office; I knew of his vile intentions to harm us and would not allow that. Everybody returned to their tasks, except Frank, who opted, just in case, to stay with me in the backyard, calming me down, without success.

Diego was right: in a mere five minutes, everybody heard the noise of the car approaching our driveway and the doorbell. Colonel Beltran was at the door. I continued with my incessant barking and jumping, but I was less effective from the backyard, unable to reach him. Otherwise, I would show him who is protecting this house.

"You owe me a bottle of rum," said Diego to Mommy Dora.

To make my story short, I believe my warnings had the desired effect because, after ten or fifteen minutes of my extra loud protests, I heard how Colonel exited the house and left in his car. When I was allowed back into the house, I found our embarrassed team and a small crowd of tourists near the house wandering at my insane barking. Some were even trying to climb up our backyard fence, curious to see what provoked my barking. Probably, they all came to congratulate me for successfully scarring and expelling the enemy without excessive violence or publicly offensive behavior. That is, of course, thanks to God, none of them understands my dog language.

Mommy said to Diego that I went mad, and, in the future, they would have to take me far away to the beach before Colonel Beltran comes. It means the Colonel should not come again to our office without a reasonable warning. The little she knows; it makes no difference where I will be at the time. I will immediately feel the enemy's approach independent of distance because I sense the danger nearly ten minutes before the enemy's arrival. It is indeed harder to pull my handlers on my leash when they resist, but if I feel I must urgently return from the beach to our house to protect my human pack, I will be very capable of doing that, if necessary.

Immediately after Colonel Beltran left, Fernando called at our entrance door to ask what was happening with me. You see, Fernando is my personal friend, my admirer, and very protective of me. A couple of months earlier, I even convinced him to adopt one of Pretty's pups from her second litter.

"I thought that someone had raided your house. What was all this aggressive barking about?" asked Fernando.

I scrolled on my tummy towards him to show my appreciation for his concern and licked his shoes to demonstrate that I was the noblest dog on this planet to everyone: human or animal, who didn't mean harm to my human pack. Of course, he surrendered 'tout-suit' and started petting me, still worried.

"What happened to Benz?" he repeated his question.

"Inexplicable," said Mommy Dora. "Never before Benz acted like that. Colonel Beltran is the only visitor at whom Benz ever barked. Actually, he started the annoying, aggressive commotion and growling even ten minutes before Colonel Beltran arrived. Frank removed Benz to the backyard, but it didn't help. Benz disobeyed Frank and continued with obsessive barking, enabling our visitor to talk. Colonel Beltran was spooked, visibly scarred, and had to leave."

"Who is your visitor? Has he ever come here before and had an incident with Benz?" asked Fernando. "That could explain the animosity between them."

"He is the military boss, who overtook our Cuban partner in our Joint Venture, to express it mildly, in an unfriendly way. We were not informed of what took place and never met with him before. According to Diego, last week Colonel Beltran came here without warning once before while we were away at the meeting with you, but he had to leave without entering because Benz was barking aggressively".

"Esta volao, tumba eso y manten tu laton con tapa!" (It's amazing, don't share it with anyone, keep the lid on it!) said surprised Fernando. "This man and his people are too powerful. It is better not to know about this incident. Stay safe; I haven't heard anything", added Fernando and left.

Meanwhile, the rest of our pack came down from the second-floor office to pet me and show me their solidarity. They said that I must be careful because if reported to Zoonosis by the Colonel as an aggressive and dangerous dog, their monster track might arrive to arrest me and kill me. Mommy and daddy didn't help our apprehension when they shared with us the content of their brief discussion with the Colonel, who informed them that all Cuban employees would have to resign until they are screened to determine their reliability for contracting them with the Cuban Navy.

Those who the Navy can not employ will be substituted by the existing navy personnel. All foreign employees of the International Economic Association (IEA) will also have to undergo a new screening for their working visas. Their working permits and our current Cuban research ship operation will require new Navy permits. All these procedures will cost additional fees charged to IEA.

Every team member, including me, after this briefing, felt even more worried. In my case, I was worried about Zoonosis for dogs which, as I heard before, kill their canine victims with extreme cruelty. In the case of human pack members, they were worried about Zoonosis for humans, which will fire them from their jobs in IEA.

"Don't you worry," I tried to tell my human pack, "I will fight for all of us and fulfill my job of protecting you, our office, and our ship from all the dangers!"

Little did I know, but these despicable assassins of dogs Zoonosis from Havana came to Tarara with their death wagon a few days later. They kidnapped all those poor dogs they found on the streets of Tarara. Gogi and I survived only thanks to Fernando, who came to warn us of the forthcoming slotter. He said that Havana's Zoonosis called him in the morning to inform him that they had another complaint about Benz, and they were coming to wipe the streets and the beach of Tarara from all dangerous dogs. Fernando argued with Zoonosis that such dogs could not be found in Tarara. What was needed is the waste collection and washing of the streets to prevent infections from the long-term unremoved trash containers, but they said they were ordered by the military authorities to wipe out dogs.

Fernando was certain that this order came from our recent visitor Colonel Beltran. Frank and Dora immediately hid Gogi and me in the secret bunker below our house. They knew about this secret bunker because our Cuban friends asked permission to drill its walls, hoping to find the hidden treasures of its previous owner Carlos Prío Socarrás. They never found anything but made a lot of noise and garbage with their electric drill.

Meanwhile, Diego ran to the beach searching for Pretty. It was a futile effort. Zoonosis came in less than ten minutes later with their monster truck carrying huge jaws on its rear. It swallowed all poor canine victims dragged by the horrible long poles of dog catchers, not only from the streets but even from the unfenced backyards of their owners. Diego returned worried; he didn't manage to find Pretty.

So cruel. Pretty was less than two years old, healthy, and very smart. If she would have been staying at home, she would be hidden with us and could be saved. But I guess she was not properly warned of the mortal danger canine freedom represents in Cuba. Anyway, all those dogs that Zoonosis caught, never mind from where they were caught in their own unfenced backyards, or the beach, or the streets, they never made it back. When Dora inquired, Zoonosis refused to talk about them. They answered Dora that they had no records of any dogs since all have been already killed by strychnine.

Gogi and I didn't witness this vicious slotter personally because we were hidden in the bunker of Carlos Prío Socarrás, but we heard the accounts of those who witnessed it. Zoonosis left our Tarara traumatized. Its streets, its beaches were now all empty of all stray dogs. Actually, I knew of only one survivor, besides Gogi and me - another foreign dog, a German Sheppard of a Cuban/French couple, who were like us, warned by Fernando and hid their dog in a safe location inside their house. After that, we, the survivors, were not allowed to go out for a walk at all, even on a leash.

I had to recognize the full defeat of my well-intentioned effort. Neither I was able to protect the dogs of Tarara from Zoonosis for Dogs, nor I could defend our IEA from the military takeover by Zoonosis for Humans. Of course, in my good Cuban tradition, when asked who is guilty, I always answer with a popular Cuban aphorism: *'La culpa tienen totis'* (Totis are the guilty).

Chapter 12

Our human pack is not so worried about us, dogs, as they are worried about their employment with the IEA and their working visas. "It is all your fault, Bez," they growled. They all know that the Cuban military took over our Joint Venture, not because of mi. I overheard our humans saying that the Cuban military overtook more than sixty percent of the Cuban economy in general. Mommy Dora and Daddy Frank spoke to their lawyer, who advised them to appeal before officially complaining. To that end, Mommy wrote an official letter soliciting a meeting with Colonel Beltran and copied this letter to a Cuban state lawyer overseeing the IEA. In response, Colonel set a morning meeting with Dora and Frank in his office in Havana a couple of days later.

Overhearing my parents talking about it in our bedroom motivated me to sneak out from the bunker after mommy took us there the following day in a hurry and haven't properly locked its door. I jumped into the van and hit myself under its back seat in an audacious attempt to travel with Mommy Dora and Daddy Frank for their protection during their meeting with Colonel, but I was discovered.

"What the hell you are doing under this seat, Benz? How did you sneak out of the bunker? Get out of here."

"No, I will not leave, don't you see that I need to come with you! Protecting you is my job. Colonel Beltran will destroy all of us and steal all our food if I don't scare him. I know it," I barked, but they didn't understand my canine vocals.

"Silly dog, stop barking, get out of here back into the bunker. You must hide there before someone notices you and reports you to Zoonosis again. Diego, please drag him out and lock him in a bunker. See that the bunker with Benz and Gogi is locked well this time, please."

"How rude. Why can't I drive with my human parents, Diego? I did that before many times. I am not a dangerous dog, but my parents are going to meet a dangerous man. I know of his intentions and the need to prevent the damage. I don't want to suffer the same as my friend, the German Shepard Guapo. Don't push me, don't lock this door!" I protested when Diego refused to listen and dragged me back into the bunker.

No, my efforts were useless; they left for the meeting in Havana without me. Worried and feeling helpless, I experienced an anxiety tantrum. Finally, Vera took pity on us and took us inside the house, where she comforted us in a bedroom filled with the scent of our adoptive parents. Mommy Dora and Daddy Frank returned much faster than expected. They looked sober and worried.

"What happened, guys?" inquired our surprised teammates.

"Frank sent Colonel to hell, and we left the meeting," murmured Mommy Dora.

"Are you in your mind?" someone asked in shock.

"We just lost it when Colonel Beltran pinned us on the low seats in his office and hovered above both of us, physically demanding our complete and immediate obedience. He also demanded additional payment for our permits and for his people, whom he would send to work with us shortly to substitute for you guys. When I asked about their qualifications for the job, Colonel Beltran said that it wasn't important because we would need to train them in the use of our equipment anyway. We refused to discuss any changes in the personnel because we have already trained you guys to work with us, and we are satisfied with your performance. Frank pointed out that if the working permits are not issued, it will become the legal reason to claim the breach of contract by the Cuban party, for which Cuba will have to compensate a foreign partner," recounted Mommy Dora.

"After that, Colonel Beltran jumped all over me," said Daddy Frank. "He was shouting that he regards our disobedience as sabotage. Probably this is how he treats his soldiers. He said that he attempted to visit us twice, but we converted our office into a trap where he was attacked by a murderous animal. Colonel's loud shouts were so ridiculously offensive, whimsical, and provocative that I had no choice but to push him aside to be able to walk out through the door outside. We left without saying goodbye."

"During our drive back," said Mommy Dora, "we discussed this untenable situation and decided that urgent help from our high-level Cuban patron was needed."

I don't understand this Colonel Beltran; why he bites the giver's hand while asking for more food. Of course, I am only a dog, and you will never find a dog stupid like that. The terror attacks will only result in the escape of their victims and never in collaboration. How in hell, we, dogs, can escape if dogs can't learn to scuba dive to Florida!

That evening Mommy Dora called her Cuban patron - a soft-spoken gentleman, Comandante Tainted, who brought her to Cuba in the first place. She implied that IEA is in very serious trouble and invited Comandante Tainted and his family for dinner next weekend to discuss the current situation. When I attempted to cheer everybody up by performing my traditional spinning and skating on the marble floor, they acted annoyed instead of amused and left the office.

"Stop you, troublemaker, all this spinning; you will break furniture in the hall. Stay quiet because we need to find the right arguments to protect you from accusations of being a murderous dog. We all know that you would never bite anyone, not even cricket or toti, but we need to be more creative in this case to make you irreplaceable in the IEA," said Mommy Dora.

"Nobody doubts that I am irreplaceable. Why else the ogre wanted to crop my ears and dock my tail! Look at my emblem of Mercedes Benz! I never heard of any other dog licensed by the Mercedes Benz," I barked, but nobody again understood me.

"Well, remember about a personal favor Comandante Tainted asked us about? Let's think about it," suggested Daddy Frank.

"Comandante Tainted told us that Fidel Castro personally delegated him to find the lost treasures of the Cathedral de Merida hidden in one of the numerous caves of Guanahacabibes," said mommy.

"Wait a minute, dear, it was also rumored that Comandante Tainted already conducted two large expeditions into those caves with the assistance of Cuban Revolutionary Arm Forces, but they found nothing. What we heard about those expeditions was embarrassing for Comandante Tainted. The military techs provoked a full collapse of the roof in one of the caves when exploding dynamite," interrupted her Daddy Frank.

O, yes! The caves are an interesting proposition, Mommy, I thought. *My predecessors: wolves and dogs, lived together with humans in caves for thousands of years. This is why we wolves and dogs can see in total darkness and know what is going on by sniffing scent. What my predecessors learned is recorded in the hard disk of my snout. For sure, I can locate the wildlife and the objects in the cave; I love digging in the ground and probably will enjoy searching the caves. The only part I don't understand is about that dynamite. When I dig, I am careful not to damage my precious bones or objects under the ground. Clearly, humans are not that smart.*

"Remember Frank, when we said to Comandante that our magnetometer is effective only in water, he arranged for our search permit in the coastal waters near his treasure caves in the hope that some of these treasures also sunk to the ocean bottom in a battle with the pirates. Maybe we could try to convince Comandante Tainted that Benz has a unique value for his project because he can catch the scent of hidden treasures," Mommy continued in sync with me.

Yes, I could find the scent of treasure if I could smell its sample before the search. Boy, I love it already, I thought.

"Let's see, maybe we should train Benz to search?" suggested mommy. "We need to investigate if he can learn to do it. We must experiment with him in search and find."

"How will you train him in treasure search, Dora?" asked Daddy Frank. "Even if it is possible, it will take time. We need an immediate solution now. Of course, if by miracle, Benz could find the treasures for Comandante Tainted instead of beach garbage, it would be probably exactly what we need to get rid of Colonel Beltran."

"I bet you Benz can find treasures if there are any. He is so smart, smarter than many humans I know. How about starting in the bunker of Carlos Prio Sacarras? Shall we dig there? All Cuban team members always said that meter-thick concrete walls of the bunker and its floor should have hidden treasures," suggested Diego with enthusiasm.

"Let's not get ahead of ourselves," said Mommy Dora. "Start with his learning the scent of gold objects. We will hold Benz inside the house while you, Diego, bury these objects in a garden in the backyard. Let us start with using my gold earring."

"When I served in Angola with the Cuban army, we had 'the Russian mine-searching dogs finding the hidden explosives. That saved a lot of our lives. Could we train Benz to do something similar?" suggested Diego.

"Forget explosives, Diego. No, we don't want any," said Daddy Frank. "Now I recall how some time ago I read something about mining dogs trained in Finland or Norway... I will find more information about that."

This will be fun, I thought and bit hard with my tail in excitement against the floor. I wanted to join Diego in the backyard to see what he was doing, but Daddy Frank grabbed my collar to hold me in the kitchen, preventing me from snooping on Diego.

"Benz, Benz, come here, Search and Find," finally invited Diego, opening for me the kitchen door into the backyard.

Here I am, happy to search and find what you have hidden, but do you have my reward ready? It would be especially nice if the reward will be meat or chicken, I thought.

"Search Benz, Find!" Diego repeated his command.

I need no invitation from Diego, do you think I am stupid? All I need is to check the ground with my nose. Don't you know that we dogs can smell the scent from as far as twelve- or fifteen meters underground and even in the water? Here you go! I can smell meat; I am tracking it now. It is freshly buried underground.

Oh, it is meat; let me dig it up. Yum! This meat is good. It is a perfect game. Diego is using meat and not gold; it is perfect! Can we play it again? I thought.

Instead, I was expelled back into the kitchen.

Maybe Vera wants me now to find another piece of meat hidden in the kitchen. I know where it is – in the refrigerator.

No such luck; Vera does not want to play. All my efforts to convince her that this is an important part of my learning search haven't moved her a bit. Diego returned to the kitchen, and said 'sniff', he gave me to sniff one of Gogi's toys. After that, he left for the garden in the backyard again but came back for me in a few minutes. He saved Vera from my nudging by finally leading me to the backyard.

"Search Benz, find," he repeated the same command as before. I sniffed the air for meat. *Nothing in the backyard! I am confused. Let me sniff the ground in all corners; probably, it is where Diego hid it. No, there is no scent of meat, but I shall check this freshly dug ground in a corner just in case. It is a disaster...*

Instead of meat, I am pulling a toy, one I sniffed before. It was hidden in the ground beside the fence. That is cheating, Diego; I can't eat this; it is not fair.

"Good Benz, bravo, here is your treat," mommy gives me my proper meat reward for finding the toy.

Yes, I got it. I must search and find anything they give me to sniff before, and they will reward me when I find it. Who has the meat is the boss!

"Stop jumping on me Benz, this time, I want you to sniff my earring." Mommy Dora gave me to smell one of her earrings.

"No, this is no good! It stinks of dead gold metal. Why are you using that? Better if you ask me to smell and search for meat or chicken again. Or, if you really want to hide this gold metal, you call earring, rub the meat on it, and promise me more meat after I find it," I attempted to instruct my trainers on how to train me.

My humans didn't understand me until I conceded to find the dead gold metal first, and for this, I got rewarded with a piece of sausage. They repeated the same trick with Dora's earrings a couple of times.

Piece of cake. With a good, tasty reward, even a dog that is an idiot can find a freshly buried object with the scent of a given sample. I went straight on working the ground smelling it with my nose, and after I found where it was hidden, I dug it up with my paws.

"Look, Mommy, did I do well? Can I have my meat reward now?" I barked.

"Good dog! Now you must learn a new trick. You will get a meat reward only after you sit on your hind paws beside the buried object in the position of a Good Dog, ears perked up and howl," said Diego.

That was what Russian dogs in Angola did, and this was how we started my training as an ore dog. Dogs have the sniffing power to unearth the precious yellow prize if they are promised a reward. Diego believes that, probably, I am exceptionally talented as a search dog, and for that, I love him.

Chapter 13

Artemisa, July 1987

Now, with your permission, I would like to return to our four-hour drive from Tarara to Viñales across the region called Artemisa. We felt stressed despite the sparse car traffic on the Highway of Pinar del Rio. Our driver Gaspar had to avoid hitting all those sex-crazy dogs who run across the highway, appearing suddenly from nowhere at the speed of cruise missiles. There are also horse riders, carts towed by bulls, and numerous human hitchhikers.

The sex-crazy dogs on the highway, in particular, drove me mad. It all starts with a scared and terrorized female dog in the heat trying to escape across all six highway lines, pursuing her, the troves of dozens of imbecilic male dogs who pay absolutely no attention to the highway traffic. These idiots, of course, get run over by the cars. Drivers can't just suddenly stop their vehicles on a highway.

These poor imbeciles, slaves of sex and lust, would say that it is the fault of females in heat, but I believe, as a Holy Dog in Training should, that they deserve death for their lust and stupidity. It is we, the drivers, and passengers in cars, who are stressed to hell when driving. I felt embarrassed and traumatized.

I would never do what these imbecilic dogs do, even though I don't really know how a dog feels when having sex. Once Diego took me for a visit to his friend who had a female black Dobie in heat. Her scent was overwhelming and chaotic but wonderful. I was only six months old at that time, and she was a mature lady. I didn't know what to do with her. When I attempted to approach her aromatic sex parts, she told me to get lost; she said she wasn't ready. At first, she insulted me by calling me a large puppy because my scent was of the too-young male, not ready to fertilize her, but more important was that she didn't want to see a male yet because she needed a couple of days more enter into her estrus.

When despite her resistance, I insisted because Diego continued pushing me at her, she bit me. I run back to Diego for advice, but Diego couldn't understand her condition of being "not yet ready" and, he continued sending me back. The female Dobie became annoyed and ordered me to get off her property by biting me harder until I had to retreat behind Diego for protection. Finally, Diego understood it was useless to continue and took me back home, where he insulted me by calling me "*Bobo*" (stupid). This is totally and completely unfair because Gogi and Pretty gladly approved of his insults without listening to my explanations first.

It is not my fault that humans don't understand when a female dog becomes fertile. Humans want to control all aspects of canine life, but they don't bother to learn about our species' physiological and psychological needs. This unfortunate experience created a lasting '*Bobo* complex' in me when it had to do with sex. It is why I am a perfect candidate for Holiness.

Being full three months older than Gogi, a few months later, I tried to teach him the lecture I learned about canine sex after he confided in me about his crush on Canelita, a little stray of our Ukrainian neighbors living in Tarara's Chernobyl village. He was planning the escape from our home to meet with Canelita. I forbade him to do that and explained that he was just too young at the age of six months. But he wouldn't listen and escaped for his date with his little Canelita, a good-looking canine who might be his own older half-sister from the previous litter of Pretty stollen by Chernobyl kids.

When Vera couldn't find him at home, she panicked and went searching for him on the beach, thinking that his mother, Pretty, took him for a stride. She was wrong. Pretty much had nothing to do with it. Gogi returned later on his own and was very proud of himself. His strong, pungent, brutal smell of intercourse with Canelita was completely insulting to me. After examining him and expressing my disgust, he started walking around me with his hind legs tensed and his head and tail high. In our dog language, it is the expression of male superiority.

He proceeded to tease me, "Who is the little dog here? And who is a *bobo* here? Who is too young in this house? Ja! Well, it is not me. Can't you smell the scent I am wearing? The young baby-bobo is you, Benz! That being the case, it is me who became The Alfa Dog in this house. From now on, I will be in command! You, Benz, will have to obey me. *'El Perro Macho'* (Tough Dog) of this house is Gogi."

He was lucky indeed before I recovered from the insult and jumped him to snap his head off for such insolence. Vera entered the room and, smelling the offensive odor of Gogi, grabbed him by the scruff.

"Where have you been, little rascal? What is this horrible smell?" she said and took him for the wash with a soup in the backyard. I was waiting for him behind the door to give this insolent rascal a proper greeting with my teeth, but when Vera brought him back, he already lost the scent of Canelita and the wonderful but offensive smell of intercourse.

I thought that it would be better to forget this unfortunate matter, but Gogi continued waiting at the entrance door again for an opportunity to escape. Apparently, Vera explained to Mommy Dora after she returned home from Havana that Gogi was lusting after Canelita. Initially, mommy didn't believe her because Gogi was only six-month-old and after my fiasco, she believed he was just too young for sex. Vera explained it was normal for small breeds to enter the fertility period at the age of six months. Small breeds mature earlier than large ones. Mommy put Gogi on a leash and decided to see the owner of Canelita personally to apologize and to pay for the damage if it really took place.

Gogi happily led Mommy Dora to the Chernobyl village in Tarara because he wanted to see Canelita again, but they couldn't find her anywhere outside on the street. Mommy allowed Gogi to search for Canelita, and of course, Gogi found her house. Mommy spoke with her owner, who said that Canelita was already taken to the local veterinarian the same day to get spayed. After Mommy compensated the owner for the damage, Gogi returned home very sad and disappointed because he didn't see Canelita. When he met with her on a later occasion, Canelita did not emit a delicious pungent inviting smell and was no longer interested in him. As a consequence, from that moment on, we were treated like delinquents, not allowed to approach the entrance door without strict supervision. Again, this serves him well, but it is still completely unfair to me. I didn't do anything, even when Diego took me to the older Dobie of his friend. So, do you think Gogi learned his lesson, the way I learned mine? No, he continued annoying me with his stupid *machismo* and calling me *Bobo*, but that is another discussion we must have later.

When Comandante Tainted and Giovanni mentioned that I might become a member of their team working for the Cardinal Secretary of State of The Holy See, I understood how my previous unhappy experience with sex was my very destiny in preserving my chastity. There is no other way if I am aspiring to become a Holy Dog! Clerical celibacy is mandated for all Catholic clergy. So, I intend to behave as mommy said, as a Church servant and not as a stupid dog, and stay clear of lustful sin. Apart from that, I would never subject an innocent human driver to the similar scare and guilt of accidental killing or badly harming sex-driven, brainless canine missiles shot across highways, slaves to the overwhelming sex lust. It is disgusting and dangerous for dogs and people traveling in cars. The Holy Dog would never do that!

All those unfinished overpasses made another confusing impression on me to nowhere overlooking the highway. Their huge, tall, corroded metal and concrete structures built over six lanes of the highway have no entrance up the ramp or exit down the ramp anywhere. They are towers over the highway leading to nowhere.

When Giovanni asked Gaspar why leaving the overpasses unfinished and hanging over the six ways highways, not connecting with the ground on either side, Gaspar answered that it was Comandante en Jefe Fidel Castro's ingenious plan to mislead the invasion of the enemy. When the invaders parachute down from their helicopters to the overhanging overpasses, they will get stuck high over the ground, unable to get down. Geovanni laughed, maybe because of the ingenuity of their Comandante en Jefe or maybe because it was a funny joke, I don't know. It is hard for a dog to understand this kind of human humor.

While driving, Gaspar told us that the Cordillera de Guaniguanico is divided into the easterly Sierra del Rosario and westerly Sierra de Los Organos. From the highway, we could only see the flat and very fertile fields with colored minerals valleys sparkled with steep-sided limestone hills (*mogotes*).

"Unfortunately," said Gaspar, "these are only the tobacco plantations. They replaced all other crops here. That is because its naturally rich mineral red soil produces the very best tobacco, and the Cuban state considers tobacco more profitable for hard currency sales abroad than the food."

I wasn't interested in tobacco, for I hate its smell, it stinks of hell, but the area is unique and beautiful! The fields of different distinct colors are surrounded by blue mountains. When we finally took a turn at the city of Pinar Del Rio and arrived at the house reserved for the state visitors near Viñales, known as the karst depression of Cuba, I couldn't believe my eyes. I have never seen anything similar; the natural surroundings were nothing like the coastal sandy mangroves - my home.

The huge blue and green elevations called Rosario Mountain Range among the valleys of tobacco fields, rivers, and forests have an ideal landscape due to fertile red mineral sedimentation soil plowed by oxen to cultivate special red crops.

We need immediately investigate these new hunting grounds even before we will start our cave hunting in Guanahabibes! I was thinking.

"Not so fast," said Gaspar after I got out of the car and pulled with all my might towards magotes. These were very strange high singular natural green domes I have never seen before. "We will stroll outside a bit later," he said, "first, we leave the luggage in our rooms and have a snack."

The state visitors' house is very nice, and its service people greeted us very friendly, but I was impatient and worried about wasting daylight before hunting. I continued pulling my leash, very excited, and anxious to go outside.

"Your snacks are served in the dining room," announced the servant.

Diego ordered me to shut up and let him enjoy the food, for it is a very special opportunity for him, currently available in Cuba only for prestigious visitors, hard currency tourists, and dignitaries of the Cuban state.

What? What is it? The smell!' The strong smell of barbequed pork waiting for us at the table in the dining room hit my snout. The barbequed pork smells irresistible, forget hunting, forget anything else, and give me the barbequed pork, please... We Cubans are ready to die for barbequed pork; we prefer it to anything else.

"Here, Benz," Diego called me to the table, following Gaspar and Giovanni. The servants poured my water into a bowl left on the floor beside the table and the refreshing drinks for my human companions. We were served *Calzones Cubanos* – delicious Cuban biscuits with slices of barbequed pork, ham, and pickles. After these delicious snacks, we, I included, felt like having a nap. However, Gaspar led everyone outside to allow us to walk a bit before the dark and have at least a quick view of this special landscape. We walked towards nearby Magote del Valle.

The local guide - a geologist, who accompanied us, explained,

"The mountain range is called Cordillera de Guaniguanico," explained the local guide - a geologist, who accompanied us. "It consists of limestone and metamorphic rock. You can also observe magotes - the huge singular karst hammocks with tall vertical walls made of karstified limestone reaching up to six hundred meters in height above sea level, strung along flat plains of tobacco valleys. The limestone medium becomes karstified only when aggressive waters flow through it. It is a process of karstification by the enlargement of pores.

"In the rocky massifs of the Oligocene period, it created domes of limestone mounds which are usually full of caves. They are famous for tourists and boat tours along its subterranean rivers floating through limestone caves inside magotes. Numerous spices from the Mesozoic Age can be found in fossil forms. In addition to mollusks, there are exclusive species of reptiles and amphibians. Large paleontological plots with Jurassic and Quaternary fossils are inside its caverns and outside, among which are the ancient fish."

It is confusing for a dog. I don't understand what it means the Oligocene period, the Mesozoic Age, and the Jurassic

and Quaternary fossils, too many fancy names for me, I thought. Thankfully, Gaspar didn't know either and asked the guide, who answered that the geology of Cuba was formed in the Oligocene geologic period thirty-four to twenty-three million years ago. And the Jurassic and Quaternary fossils are related to 0.5 -2.0 million years ago.

Too far back in time for me. I can't count such large numbers. All I want is to hunt inside the cave of magote, I thought. Still, it sounds like exciting hunting! I would love to find reptiles, amphibians, and fossils in caves. It is my domain, my nature, and my predecessor – the wolf is already awakening in me. Let's go inside the caves of magotes, so I can show off my talents!

Instead, the geologist continued lecturing us at the base of *magote*, "The local caverns and cave networks are created inside *magotes* when carbon dioxide is present in water. It affects the limestone rocks dissolving them. The porous rocks subjected to this 'aggressive water' can completely lose their consistency by reducing the cohesion between the grains and crystals that make them up."

The explanations from the guide are too long for me; all I wanted was to investigate the closest to us, the cave Cueva del Vaca. The beautiful sunset already started coloring the skies, and I was apprehensive that it would become too late to start our cave tour. I became agitated and impatient, which usually results in my barking. Careful not to ruin my reputation with Giovanni, I restrained myself from barking this time.

"We don't have daylight time for an expedition into the caves of *magote* today," added the guide. "I could book for tomorrow morning the equipment required for touring caves, that's if you are interested and can spend a day with us tomorrow."

"Sure, we are interested, but unless Giovanni decides otherwise, tomorrow we will have to proceed in a hurry to Guanahacabibes, where other members of our scientific team have already arrived to work with us on a project" apologized, Gaspar.

"In Viñales, we have hundreds of different caves with spectacular gigantic columns, stalagmites, stalactites, mantles, and underground streams that, due to the season, run fast and abundant. I hope you can stop at least for a day in this temple of nature on your return trip," the guide was promoting the wonders of Viñales professionally.

The only reason I agreed to return to our state visitor's house was my memory of delicious, barbequed pork biscuits served before. On our return, we were served *mojitos* (Cuban fresh mint cocktails) and hors d'oeuvre. I was given only cold water, but I tasted some hors d'oeuvre, many of them are just with shellfish, and I liked them less than the main dish with *'Lechon Asado'* – made with slow barbequed pork, which Diego and I enjoy the most.

Giovanni also loved its moist, sweet taste, and Gaspar explained to me how it takes six hours to barbecue in low temperatures this most loved traditional Cuban dish. Of course, I was interested in pleasing my new pack, so I decided to show off my usefulness as a search dog and a protector by sniffing the air in our adjoining bedrooms as soon as we retired.

Diego was staying with me in my bedroom while Giovanni and Gaspar each got their own. I heard, investigated, and immediately found from where an unusually funny, high frequencies hum was coming. It was coming from under the floor at the joint wall with the room of Geovanni. I sat down on my hind legs at the location emitting these high frequencies hum, and after a while, being frustrated that nobody appreciated my warning, I howled, indicating that I found from where this hum was coming. Diego didn't understand me and tried to calm me down, but Gaspar came into our bedroom and said that he would have to remove me from Diego's room to his own room because I am disturbing our prestigious guest with my howling, which obviously, according to him, originated from my sensing rats or other rodents.

"This is bullshit, Gaspar," I tried to protest, but he took me to his bedroom and closed his door, then he scolded me, "'*Coñoo'* (damn), don't you create an international incident here with your devilish snout, especially after you have eaten this evening as a King. You are just too stupid to understand what you must ignore if you want to continue eating like this. Don't ever try again to search our bedrooms unless I tell you otherwise. From now on, all search orders will be mine."

Then he called someone in Havana to report the incident, "Reduce the power for activating the listening bugs, please. This crazy dog with his long atomic snout has already detected the electronic bugs in the wall and formed the scandal by howling at them. We are risking upsetting our guest if he will interpret the barking of the dog as a warning."

I don't understand Gaspar, I was thinking. Which bugs? What kind of bugs? I usually eat only those bugs who molest me. No, he called them electronic bugs. I never met an electronic humming bug before. Long live, long learn. Why does he wants me to find the gold but doesn't want to find the bugs with high-frequency sound? Is it because they are not made of gold? Why does he want an ore-dog but not a radar-dog? According to Daddy Frank, this is how some dogs were called in England during the 2WW because they could hear the approaching enemy aircraft before any radars could. I don't get it; people could be very stupid.

By the way, my snout is not devilish. It is my Holy. Gaspar is too stupid to understand it. Mommy said that my sense of smell is a million times stronger than humans, and I can determine the direction of smell with precision at a distance dozens of times larger than humans can. Nothing devilish, it is called evolution, and it helps me to hunt.

Maybe one day in the future, humans will evolve as well, but so far, they have a long way to go.

However, I detected the signals of high-frequency signals, just like English dogs do, thanks to my hearing ability, not my smelling talents. Mommy said that we dogs can hear much more and better than humans. Humans normally hear only up to twelve thousand Hertz and only in rear cases twenty thousand Hertz, while we dogs can hear a frequency range up to sixty thousand hertz. Not only can we hear it, but with our special ear eighteen muscles that control the ear flap, we can tune the position ear canal to localize the sound accurately and from really far away, dozens of times further than humans can. Unfortunately, it also means that the loud noises tolerated by humans may be scary and painful to dogs. Humans don't understand that and often blast their motors, vacuum cleaners, music, or other loud noises in the presence of dogs. It is very painful for dogs. Humans say they love us, but they don't care to learn how we are different from them and what will cause us serious stress and pain.

I want to say that if humans can't hear these noises, it doesn't mean they don't exist. I could easily distinguish that this time the noise came not from the rodents but from the electromagnetic pulses. Still, I am not stupid and know how to take my orders from the alfa man. In our case, he is Gaspar, not Diego. I must obey Gaspar if I want to help my family pack. After all, it is not such a big sacrifice. I prefer cave hunting in nature to hiding in the bunker of Carlos Prio Socarras in Tarara from Zoonosis! With these thoughts, I slept without further incidents and, after breakfast, boarded our station wagon to travel to Guanahacabibes.

Chapter 14

Thankfully, the next morning I was allowed to sit with Diego because Gaspar had to drive. It is clear that the alfa male in our small pack here, without a doubt, is Gaspar. I was ordered to follow his commands before anybody else. To tell you the truth, after last night, I became apprehensive about Gaspar for him being rude, bossy, and not affectionate with me, the way everybody else was. Also, I am aware that Diego is scared of Gaspar due to my acute ability to read even the slightest emotions of others. Geovanni is the only happy and relaxed soul in our pack, probably because he leaves the burden of decision-making to Gaspar. After all, he knows that while I am protecting him, there is nothing to worry about. I will do my best not to disappoint him. When we arrived at this Unesco-declared Biosphere Reservation, the Guanahacabibes Peninsula, and part of the Sierra del Rosario Mountain Range, I understood why UNESCO declared it a World Heritage Site.

I prefer the road of Luis Lazo from Viñales to Guane better than the highway from Havana because it has only two lines. We haven't seen on this road yet a single suicidal dog. Of course, maybe it was just too early in the morning. Still, in my opinion, it is much more interesting and beautiful because it crosses the Sierra de Los Organos, the rivers, the forest, and several small villages. We arrived at Guane, known as Nueva Pilipina, approximately an hour. Geovanni wanted to see the church of Guane and, if possible, to meet with Bishop Jose Siro Gonzales, head of the Catholic Church in Pinar del Rio.

Unfortunately, Gaspar decided that my presence at their meeting was out of the question. Geovanni and Gaspar went into the church for the meeting on their own while Diego and I went for a walk around this small town, made up only of two streets lined up with some small, old, rustic houses. It is located on the right bank of the Cuyaguateje River, close to numerous rich tobacco fields and mountains.

It looks like a town of the stone age. Guane is poor, with houses built of the materials commonly used for construction in old times, such as wood, guano (seabirds and bats excrements), yagua (fibrous tissue from the wood of the royal palm), and muddy (mud with rubble). Some masonry constructions (stone with lime and clay mortar) and houses are made of bricks with shingle roofs, but the village church is the only architectural work of importance. It's one of those lifeless towns, as people say—a lot of poverty.

Just like every small Cuban town does, it has a *Bodega* store where humans go with their ration booklets to get some essentials they need (very few of them usually are available). Their rations, I was told, should last for ten days. Guane also has a primary school and one family doctor, an undersupplied butcher, and a dirty, chaotic farmer's market in the same condition as the butchers, a state-run café in the same shape. A drugstore where medicines are in shortage; a workshop where electrical appliances are repaired despite the shortage of spare parts.

However, the people here are the best thing about this place. I made numerous friends on the street; many of them, especially children, stopped to pet me. I liked them instantly. They are humble, without a bad bone in their bodies—the kind of people who share everything they have with you. In short, good people. Of course, there are also a few bad apples like anywhere else in the world. Just to show that I am a working dog, I sniffed both streets and the riverbank for hidden treasures but found none. When Gaspar and Geovanni came back from their meeting that lasted more than an hour, they called us, and we returned to the car to continue our drive to the most western region of Cuba – Guanahacabibe.

"We learned a few interesting details from our meeting with the Cuban Obispo of Pinar del Rio," said Geovanni. "The first church dedicated to San Idelfonso was built of very rustic local materials: *'yagua y el guano'*. It was erected in Sansueña - six kilometers away from the village itself and transferred closer to the village when its structure started to fall apart. Its second structure was also built of guano and had to be transferred closer to the village to its present location on top of the hill.

"Two years later, this second one collapsed, and the wooden church was built. Cuban forces of General Maceo burned this church and the rest of the village during the war of Independence in 1896, but the body of the church and its tower remained standing. In 1901 the church was rebuilt of stone, creating one of the best structures in the entire territory of *'Vuelta Abajo'* (Turning Down), the name for the region of Pinar Del Rio in those times.

"The church in its current form was rebuilt in 1950, mainly due to the efforts of its priest Rolando Lara, who transformed the old church into a regional icon. Actually, it is still a most impressive ancient structure built of adobe in Pinar del Rio.

"Another interesting detail was about the escape of its priest Father Rios when General Antonio Maceo occupied Guane in 1896. Father Rios transported the church records to the town of Luis Lazo, through the mountain range, using his donkey to save these records from possible destruction, for the church was actually used as barracks by the Spanish and was burned down by the Cuban forces of General Maceo. The First Volume of church records had the record of the death of white humans in Nueva Filipina, including the death of a frier from the Cathedral of San Ildefonso de Merida. Currently, it is in possession of the Vatican."

Interesting story, I thought, *but to be honest, I don't trust anything unless I find its scent. Why don't we look for the scent in caves instead of all this talking?*

The road to La Bajada, an obligatory checkpoint of the Cuban Coast Guard equipped with a large marine radar installation, from where we have to start our adventure, is even more interesting than the highway. It is a single two-way road with lots of horse-drawn traffic and the odd stray cow between the small villages of rangers and fishermen.

"Semi-dry forest of precious cedar wood and mangroves cover much of the landscape on both sides of the road, providing important habitat for deer, wild pigs, and iguanas," said Gaspar.

A couple of times, I had an irresistible impulse to jump from the car window to chase some of these animals when used to the car traffic, they paid little attention to the car traffic and continued with their business. Unfortunately, our car windows were closed; all I could do was helplessly bark at them. To forget this frustration, I started listening to endless stories of Gaspar about the old legends and people of the peninsula.

"The absence of fertile soil, very limited access to fresh water, and plagues of insects, especially mosquitos and, most of all, the angry sandflies, prevented the Spanish colonizers from settling in Guanahacabibes. Before Spanish colonizers, the peninsula was the home of the peaceful aboriginals Guanahatabeys. Their name for the peninsula Guanahacabibes could be interpreted as a place of the iguanas or site of the iguanas: Guana (Iguana), ha (yes), cabibes (site or place). The aboriginals benefited from territories with abundant forests, caves, desirable land, and marine food; they left many archaeological sites throughout the peninsula," explained Gaspar.

"Then in the sixteenth, seventeenth, and eighteenth centuries came the pirates, corsairs, and privateers to establish their secluded service bases and hide their fleet for the obvious geographical strategic position of this territory and the isolation of the area, with very little human activity at the time. The majority of current residents of the peninsula are their descendants. They are mostly fishing, hunting, timber cutting, charcoal burning, and honey producing.

"Did you say the charcoal burning? Do you mean the coal mines?" asked Geovanni.

"No, we don't have the coal produced by nature, so we are producing it by ourselves out of wood and shrubs, such as Ebony charcoal that grows on the coastal karst, but it is rare to find large trees. They have straight, few centimeters, thin trunks, and loose bark. The heart of this plant is an intense black color, very heavy and compact. They also slow burn other wild trees and shrubs, such as the maribu shrubs, to produce the coal, but this is a very hard and slow job," answered Gaspar.

"Numerous ingenious legends are narrated here about the local caverns. For example, they say that two majas (Cuban snakes) for many years live in Cueva la Sorda," continued Gaspar. "The legend tells that they are not poisonous. They are two young people who turned into snakes a long time ago by a curse of their own father. There are also many stories about the Black Maroons (runaway blacks), who escaped from their masters and hid in the caves of Cabo de San Antonio, but these stories I will tell you later because we almost arrived at La Bajada."

This sounds like an interesting but also challenging ground for hunting, I thought. Finally, we arrived at the coastal control center La Bajada – a Coast Guard military checkpoint with a large marine radar installation permitting detection of all marine traffic, even when invisible. They have a funny name for what they do. For the tourist's convenience, they are called a visitors center.

Everyone submitted their passports for registration, except mine. Diego claimed me as his dog, while he knows that I would prefer to be registered as a foreign dog with Giovanni as my master.

You see, it is an important advantage in Cuba to be registered as a foreign dog, the same as in Tarara, I would get better treatment if I could share the foreign tourists' accommodations with my foreign master, and good food from the restaurant. The guards checked our papers and luggage and permitted us to drive for another fourteen km to Maria La Gorda, a small hotel for foreign tourists pertaining to the Cuban military chain of resorts and hotels Gaviota. It is located on the coast of Cabo Corrientes of Bahia Corrientes.

By the gravel road along the coast of the peninsula, we arrived at Maria La Gorda, consisting of twenty houses: bungalows and two stories of concrete condo units, a restaurant, a bar, and a dive center with a few peers for the boats. The ocean was sparkling emerald green at the coast, changing its color to deep blue further on the horizon. The surrounding green forest and white silica sand of the beach sparkled with palm trees, making it look like an idyllic scuba diving paradise with the famously rich coral reefs and fabulous fishing, but very soon we understood why it was and still is very scares in population.

On arrival, we got out of the car to look at the beach and stretch our legs. The angry mosquitos and swarms of mad sandflies attacked every inch of our exposed skin. These aggressors are much worst here than those of Tarara. My unprotected skin was viciously attacked by the swarms of sandflies with my nose, and my ears by the dark clouds of crazy mosquitos.

Giovanni and Gaspar carried their luggage to the registration center, leaving Diego and me in a car. I got scared that Diego and I will become excluded from all the perks and fun: such as protection from mosquitos, air conditioning, hunting in caverns, and food in the hotel's restaurant. I loudly protested. I was right, but Diego explained that Cubans are prohibited from staying in the hotel for foreigners in Maria La Gorda.

"What? Why not? It is about our comfort and food. Why can't Cubans stay if they could pay for it in hard currency? Will Cubans contaminate it? What nonsense! You should have registered me as a foreign dog and yourself as a handler of a foreign dog. My purpose here is to help Giovanni, a foreign emissary; he would pay for us," I barked.

"Stop barking and jumping, Benz," said Diego. I am not in charge here. Gaspar already told you who the boss was. You and I have to obey his orders."

"O yee... Why is Gaspar allowed to stay in the hotel of Maria La Gorda, but I am not? Totally unfair: I am more foreign than Gaspar!"

"Gaspar is an officer in charge of the security taking care of Giovanni, all he needs to do is to mention that Comandante Tainted already made the arrangements."

"Comandante Tainted loves me too; why didn't he send the message that I was a foreign dog? I love good food; you know that."

"It is your own fault Benz, why did you have to fuss about the hidden recording devices in Viñales? Every Cuban would suspect that the government visitor's house is equipped with such devices. Oh..., sorry, I forgot that you are a foreign dog! From now on, Gaspar will be more careful and will not allow you to stay in a hotel with Geovanni, so stop whimpering like a spoiled baby!"

"Ridiculous! Where are we going to eat? Or to sleep? I can't sleep here without the mosquitos' screen and air conditioner in such an oppressively hot climate. The skin on my tummy is already bitten by the sand flies and my nose, my ears by the dark clouds of crazy mosquitos. Is there another hotel in all of Guanahacabibes for the Cubans?"

"We are going to stay with the Cuban scientists waiting for our arrival at Cabo de San Antonio to help in our search. They were expected to stay in '*campismo popular*' (the rustic holiday camp for Cubans) at Uvero Quemado, but the guards of La Bajada told us that their location was suddenly changed to the tent camp nearby Los Morros at Cabo de San Antonio."

"Oh..., good. At least '*campismo popular*' might have mosquitos screens, and in such hot weather, it should have an air conditioner, I hope. How will we get there? Could you start driving there? I am hungry! Will they offer us the barbequed pork in '*campismo popular*'?"

"No, Benz. I doubt they have the pork. Maybe the fish, if they caught it, but we can't drive to Cabo de San Antonio just yet. We have to wait until Geovanni and Gaspar check into their rooms and finish their lunch at the restaurant. Then Gaspar will drive all of us to Cabo de San Antonio."

"Do you think Gaspar will ask for doggie bags for me and you at the restaurant while they are having their meal?"

"I hope so; we are all hungry," answered Diego.

At this very moment, I noticed a large iguana showing her head from the nearby forest. I forgot of my hunger, mosquitos, and sand flies and jumped from the car to run into the forest after the iguana but had to drag Diego on the other end of my leash. I pulled Diego so hard that he almost lost his shoulder and let my leash go. He actually fell on his belly when in pursuit of me; he tripped on the surfacing tree root. I felt sorry and stopped to find out if he was hurt. Luckily, the silica sand covering almost everything in the area protected him from getting hurt, and he forgave me after my profuse apology and licks of his face. We went on a leash while in the forest, sniffing the tracks of iguana until the angry sand flies and mosquitoes, almost blinding us, drove us back into the car.

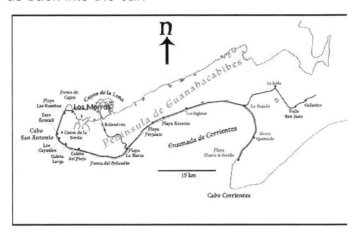

The Peninsula of Giuanahacabibes

Chapter 15

On their return, Geovanni and Gaspar brought our doggie bags containing delicious hamburgers. They also had a bottle of liquid mosquito repellant available for purchase in the hotel for foreign tourists. Diego attempted to use some of it on me, but it smelled so horrible that I understood it would kill me with its poison faster than mosquitos. I adamantly refused this repellant but accepted two hamburgers, which I ate from my dish, included in my luggage. Diego ate his hamburgers from the napkin. I was so pleased with the hamburgers that I forgave him for the error of stripping away my foreign status.

Geovani asked why the only hotel in Guanahacabibes is for foreigners. Feeling a bit sheepish, Gaspar told us a salty 'shaggy-dog story': "Keeping with Maria La Gorda's old traditions.," he said, "the name Maria La Gorda has derived from the legend. Maria, a young Venezuelan woman of generous proportions, was kidnapped and brought by the pirates to the unpopulated western coast of Guanahacabibes, where she was raped by the whole crew of a pirate ship and abandoned.

She rapidly noticed that the pirate ships hiding from the Spanish fleet in Cabo Corrientes and Cabo San Anton were lacking essential services and supplies. To survive, she became an entrepreneur and created a profitable business offering a complete 'one-stop service' to the passing pirate ships. She became a flourishing filibuster (a person engaging in unauthorized activities) and a single employer on the peninsula, providing food and prostitutes, whom she hired from the local native tribes and even some Spanish women, who were also kidnaped by the pirates and abandoned on the Guanahacabibes coast. This is how many of the residents of Guanahacabibes are the descendants of pirates and their women who settled on this coast."

Strong people, I thought. *Industrious and entrepreneurial. Just like us dogs, when we were forcibly brought to populate a new land, we found how to survive by pleasing our masters.* Suddenly, I remembered that despite my natural interest in casual sex, I agreed to become a Holy Dog and felt ashamed of my thoughts. Interesting, but Geovanni didn't show that he was ashamed of this salty story; instead, he was smiling and writing down something in his notebook.

Gaspar drove us to Cabo de San Antonio past La Bajada at low speed. He said it was necessary because he didn't want to overrun iguanas or large land crabs that often cross the road without paying any attention to the cars. Still, I suspect he drove at a slow speed because he probably also felt sleepy, the way I was after the satisfying meal. Half an hour later, near the beach, *Playa La Barca,* he called our attention to look down below from our car window at the huge, corroded metal oil tank deep grounded in the sand on this secluded beach.

"This is all that was left of the secret refuel supply base for the German submarines operating during the second world war despite the pact of cooperation with the Allies and the United States in the war declaration on the Axis powers. The United States supplied Cuba with modern military aircraft, vital for coastal defense and anti-submarine operations. It refitted the Cuban Navy with modern weapons and other equipment, hoping that Cuba will be patrolling its waters, but Batista made himself rich by secretly dealing with Germany.

German submarines were secretly provisioned in Cabo de San Antonio shores before they would return to Europe over the whole period of war due to its unique advantage: the coast of Cabo de San Antonio was secluded and unpopulated while offering the deepwater depth required by submarines near the coast. Batista furiously defended his little secret business with Germany against all persistent rumors about these German supply bases. These remains of German supply base were discovered only after Batista left Cuba," boasted Gaspar.

Geovanni and Diego appeared surprised, in particular, Geovanni, who even became emotionally excited. He commented that this was a very important story that he never heard before, and he was very impressed to see with his own eyes the remains of the Cuban secret supply base for German subs. An hour later, we passed the lighthouse of Roncali (twenty-five meters high white stone structure built by Spaniards in1849) and the modern concrete barracks of the Cuban garrison of Border Troops right next to Roncali lighthouse, the military radar, and other Cuban Coast Guard installations.

"Every ten minutes, the lighthouse emits the light signal visible at the distance of thirty kilometers, aiding the navigation across the Yucatan strait," said Gaspar.

In another half an hour and seven kilometers later, we finally arrived at Los Morros, where the Cuban scientists were waiting for us in what appeared a rustic tent camp, near the sandy indigenous green area called El Veral, which is recognized by UNESCO as a Biosphere Reserve.

"Apart from the beach pockets, the peninsula is famous for its very sharp rocks, called *'dientes de perro'* o *'seboruco'*, consisting of sharp limestone rock dissolved by the waves, underground rivers, and rain. Because instead of land, there are only rocks and mosquitoes, no one wants to reside in such harsh terrain," grunted Gaspar.

The tent camp in the interior forest has no rustic housing, only a blue plastic water tank, a *bohio* - a shelter made of palm leaves without walls with an elevated wooden floor housing kitchen and shower. A few meters away from *bohio* was a camp for five military camping tents, a long rustic table with benches built on the floor from wooden planks, and walls made of four wooden logs with palm leaves in between. The coast is a six hundred meters long shallow water bay forming the arch, which Gaspar called '*La Enseñada de Cajón',* protected by *Cayos de Leña'.* The vegetation in the background are mangroves, palms, lime, coconut trees, and thin, fragile but dense green cedar forest mixed with tropical palms, jocuma, guasima, jagueyes, acana, majagua, walnut, jobo, and ocuje with thin trunks extending behind the tent camp.

"'*Pa..que este perro*?' (Why did you bring this dog?)" was the first nasty question I heard when on our arrival and the car door got opened, allowing me to jump out of the car for a pee. This rude commentary belongs to one of the men waiting nearby for our exit from the car, who I later learned was called Alejandro. I immediately felt the hostility of this middle-aged, corpulent, tanned fellow with the military posture wearing heavy military boots, and an olive green outfit with a military type of cap. He looked surprised and disgusted. Maybe he is afraid of dogs, or he is a dog hater, then I can help him with the true reason to be afraid. I growled, "Urrrrr…Urrrr... Urrrr..."

Diego pressed my leash against his leg, "'*Buenas tardes'* (good afternoon), this is Benz; he is our treasure search dog. What is wrong with you, Benz? Stop growling." I obeyed but continued being vigilant with the olive-green man ready to jump at him if he attacks anyone in my pack.

The small team of scientists from the Speleological Group of Guaniguanico (Pinar del Rio) was waiting for us beside their tent to plan with us the search in the caverns of Cabo de San Antonio. It was Gaspar who contacted them and solicited their help. They, except three olive-green men, smiled friendly at us. Gaspar introduced Geovanni as his Italian friend, who brought us the latest metal detector model with GPS, which was not available during the previous expeditions.

Strange that Gaspar is so secretive in the introduction of Geovanni, I thought *he didn't mention The Vatican, which should have been very impressive, as it was in the case of my family.* Then he introduced Diego and Benz, explaining that we will function as a Doberman treasure search dog and his handler.

An olive-green fellow again provided us with his unsolicited opinion, "What a strange Doberman looking like a gigantic coonhound with his long ears and a tail. Is he expected to function as a search dog? I know about this dog breed is used traditionally to chase runaway blacks or Jews. Doberman should be able to distinguish by the scent if the tracks belong to blacks or Jews, but I never heard of Doberman being used as a treasure search dog."

What? Doberman can distinguish if the tracks belong to blacks, whites, or Jews? Total absurd, I thought. *Only my visual senses can distinguish the color of the skin but not my nose.*

By the way, my visual senses are quite different from humans as well. While we dogs have superior to human night vision, we can't distinguish the shades of human skin color. Then, who are the Jews? Which color do they have? Do they have a different smell from white people? If my nose could distinguish people by their skin color, then the tracking of other animals would become extremely confusing. I would need a super-brain to process all that information, for there are so many different colors in animals.

Forget it; even if I try very hard, I could not satisfy the expectations of the olive-green guy, I thought.

Gaspar replied that Diego personally trained me as an ore-search dog and that he personally witnessed how I was able to find the metal objects underground and even underwater.

Right, I thought, *I can, but not by the golden color. I do it by the gold ore scent, 'sabes'?*

Diego couldn't resist the opportunity of bragging to the military guys that he learned about the search with Russian dogs during his military service in Angola. I was pleased with his nice characterization of me as an excellent student, calling me a very smart and capable dog. He also explained to everyone why my ears are preserved instead of clipped, and my tail not being docked is a special advantage for the working dog. He said that I am normally obedient, not aggressive, and might bark only when I perceive danger.

"Benz was never trained to chase anyone, neither black nor white people," concluded Diego; looking at Alejandro, he added, "Nobody needs to worry or to be afraid of this Doberman because I will handle this dog."

I thought to myself, *Dora has an interesting saying for such type of speech: "What a violin performance!" Of course, Alejandro smells of danger, and I will resolve it later when nobody can see us.*

The Cuban team was introduced to Giovanni by Gaspar: "Meet Alejandro, our security officer, helping the Speleological Group of Pinar del Rio; Armando is a doctor in geology; Paco is a doctor in archaeology; Juan is a local forester; Mario and Arturo are the divers who will help us if needed."

Armando, tall and corpulent, is an authoritative older fellow with a tanned fair complexion and professorial appearance. Paco, pale and slender, with a noble face, is a middle-aged academic with a pleasant disposition. They wore jeans with long-sleeved shirts, boots, and caps.

I kept thinking to myself, *what these important doctors were doing here without their white gowns? All the doctors in Tarara are obliged to wear their white gowns all the time.*

Juan, the forester, is a skinny, tall, and clumsy guy, dressed like a farmer with a traditional hat made of palm leaves; he has a skin of dark clay color. Mario and Arturo are young, strong, bronzed by the sun, olive-green uniformed guys. They don't smile at us as the scientists do but smell healthy. They were observing me with curiosity; all are friendly, except Alejandro - the olive-green dog hater, who was scared of me for some hard-to-understand reason. I could clearly sense the odor of his fear and hostility toward me. His two olive-green divers didn't seem to share his fear. So, here we were, ten men and one dog forming a brand-new pack to search for ancient Mexican treasure in the remote caves of Cabo de San Antonio.

Geovanni asked who formed the Speleological Group of Guaniguanico, and Armando replied that their organization was created in 1940 by Dr. Antonio Nunez Jimenez for the exploration and investigation of geology, archaeology, paleontology, y hydrology of local caverns.

Many difficult new words and names, I thought, *I am not sure if I can remember all,* I wondered.

Geovanni only asked who Antonio Nunez Jimenez was but didn't ask what all these special fields are about. Maybe he knows that. Alejandro said that Antonio Nunez Jimenez is a personal friend of Fidel Castro and the principal scientific authority in Cuba. His explanation made it easier for us to understand the magnitude of the power of Antonio Nunez Jimenez. Good, that has explained everything.

Chapter 16

"'*Bienvenidos*' (welcome) to our rustic camp. Did you enjoy your trip?" asked Paco, the archeologist, in a warm and pleasant voice.

"Gracias, Paco, all good, still it could be shorter would you stay, as I suggested, in Uvero Quemado. You don't have here either water or electricity. The guards at La Bajada told us that instead of Uvero Quemado you set up a new camp in Los Morros. What made you change the camp location?" asked Gaspar.

"To set up camp here, closer to Roncali was my decision, Gaspar," intervened Alejandro. "When we heard that your Italian friend would accompany you to help us locate the lost treasures with a new type of metal detector, my boss recommended establishing a brand-new smaller special camp for your team of cave explorers. We got water stored in this plastic tank and the electricity by pumping the water from the batteries brought from the military base at Roncali. Let me make it clear; we were told that you would bring the latest new technology, not just a dog."

"Don't worry, Alejandro," answered Gaspar, "we brought with us as promised the latest model of a metal detector. It is in a car, and Geovanni will explain how it works and its limitations. These limitations are the reason for the search dog Benz coming with us.; he might be able to overcome the limitations of the equipment."

"My boys will help you to unload your car. We left these two tents available for your use if you need to stay or store

136

your gear. Meanwhile, wouldn't you like to join us at the table for coffee and to introduce us to your new metal detector?" asked Alejandro.

While Geovanni and Gaspar, with the help of divers, were moving and sorting out their boxes on the large table in front of the tents, my and Diego's possessions with our sleeping bags were brought inside one of the tents. By the time we were ready to join Geovanni and Gaspar in accommodating their boxes with equipment, the sea breeze calmed down, and the black swords of *'jejenes'* (sandflies) clouded all over us. Diego dragged me back inside the tent with our possessions to get the disgustingly smelling repellent lotion. Of course, the awful smell from this lotion would repel not only *'jejenes'* but any decent dog as well. I started rolling in the sand to remove it because I could not stand for such a hideous smell.

Armando took an opportunity while we were inside the tent to come inside to talk with Diego about the reason for changing the plans of the camping location,

"Just curious, we were told by Comandante Tainted that we would stay in the administration camp of Uvero Quemado, closer to the caves of interest and where the administrative cabins are built with concrete paneling and equipped with mosquitos' screens, washrooms, showers, and kitchen. Do you know why instead of Uvero Quemado, we were ordered to set up this tent camp in the middle of nowhere with no mosquito' screens, washrooms, or showers? We would have to rely on a field generator for the electricity, which, as you know, due to the shortage of fuel, has minimal capacities. I attempted to ask Alejandro these questions, but all he could answer was that these were his orders, and they are not for discussion."

"I am also surprised," answered Diego, "why we are camping here when Comandante Tainted told us that we would be staying in the administration housing of the refurnished camp of Uvero Quemado. *'Jegenes'* are really bad here, and the showers from this plastic water tank pipe will be short, plus it will be difficult to cook. I served in Angola for a couple of years, and I suspect that orders of Alejandro were made without consulting with Comandante Tainted. Sorry, I don't know their reason, and nobody said anything to Comandante or me."

"What can't you understand, *compañieros*?" suddenly, Alejandro stuck his head inside the tent. "I can tell you."

He stepped inside the tent speaking in a low voice, "Comandante Tainted is not a military man by his formation, while my superiors are, and they decided that it is not desirable for an Italian tourist to snoop around former UMAP re-education labor camp at Uvero Quemado, even after it has been cleaned up and renovated after its closure.

"'*Carrajo*', I got you, Alejandro," said Diego in an obedient low tone. "We thought that it had been converted for the use of '*campismo popular*'. I know that Comandante Tainted ordered to convert the ex-barracks of prisoners into storage rooms and renovate the administrative cabins by installing new mosquitos screens, repairing the water system and electricity, as well as painting and landscaping."

"No, Diego, to prevent any leak about UMAP camp for the labor re-education of Cuban religious clergy in Uvero Quemado, we decided to prohibit its area for foreign visitors. Actually, I must warn you, such a leak will be regarded as treason," said Alejandro. "Comandante Tainted already knows of our decision to change the camp location to Los Morros. I informed him, and he agreed that we should be careful with the Italian tourist despite the highest clearance for him."

Why are they calling Geovanni an Italian tourist? I wondered. Don't they know that Geovanni is the envoy of the biggest bosses in the Vatican: Pope Paul II and the Cardinal Secretary of State of The Holy See. What is leaking?

"Don't you worry, Alejandro. We understood; no further questions will be asked," said Diego. His face and the face of Armando suddenly became stony, blank, and lost all expression. Everyone left our tent, leaving Diego and me to sort out our possessions.

"Because of them, we are going to be eaten alive by mosquitos and sandflies, especially at night," growled Diego. The problem is that too many people today know that UMAP was the first Cuban forced labor camp for Cuban religious clergy and homosexuals. Created by Che Guevarra, it is a state secret that everybody knows. So, you have to put up with mosquito repellent; otherwise, your nose, tummy, and ears will be on fire from vicious bites by flies and mosquitos. Saves?" Diego attempted again to wipe me with the monstrously stinking repellent.

No way, I thought, *this lotion stinks worse than mosquitos. I will roll in the sand and get rid of it as soon as you look somewhere else. By the way, it is your own fault, Diego, for registering me as a Cuban dog in La Bajada. If you hadn't proclaimed me being a Cuban dog, you would be able to stay with me in Maria La Gorda as a handler of a foreign dog and enjoy all the comforts at night.*

Diego paid little attention to my complaints and spread the horribly stinking repellent all over my head, tummy, and paws. I started sneezing, and my head was spinning; it was a terror. As soon as we exited our tent, Diego joined the scientific team sitting at the table under *bohio* beside the storage of drinking water and mobile stove, waiting for the coffee to be cooked. After pouring mosquito repellant on themselves, Diego, Gaspar, and Geovanni went to supervise the accommodation of food we brought, together with the provisions already raised high above the ground to protect them from rodents, wild pigs, and ants. Camp provisions were mounted high on the wooden terrace between four tall polls beside the tent of Alejandro and his divers, who were controlling all camp food.

Seeing all of them busy, I took advantage of Diego not paying attention to me and roll myself in the sand behind the tent to remove this revolting, sickening stink of repellent from my skin. It was a suicidal attempt. The sandflies apparently noticed this removal of repellent before our humans did and attacked me in countless myriads. As soon as I got on my paws, thousands of *'jejenes'* landed upon me. I was walking in their cloud, so dark that the sun was dimmed in the sky.

According to local foresters, I committed the worst mistake in this condition, acting like a maniac. I swat *'jejenes'* while jumping and biting them with my teeth and my paws. Instead of pulling *'jejenes'* one by one together with their protruding mouth parts from my flesh, I swatted, not knowing that at the moment of annihilation, they inject their poison.

It is not my fault. I don't have the human fingers to pull them. All I could do was cry loudly and jump into the air, hoping to scare them away but no such luck. All my human companions came running to watch my performance. Diego attempted to help me with no results, and the rest of the humans were happy laughing.

Juan, the local forester, brought his bag with guava and arabo tree sticks. They built a campfire for some of these aromatic wooden sticks to be burned, very much like my Daddy Frank is burning his incense herbs sticks. "This," they said, "is the only true remedy against *'jejenes'* in the sand and mosquitoes in the forest." I lay by the campfire burning aromatic wooden sticks, and after a few minutes, *'jejenes'* lost their interest in me. I decided to stay by the campfire and even sleep there at night if and when there is no good sea breeze, which, according to Juan, will solve all my problems. As I discovered, later on, the coast of Guanahacabibes can be paradise or hell, depending on the availability of the sea breeze.

Following the coffee drinking, Geovanni unpacked his precious Garrett metal detector, which he brought with him from Italy, calling it the best and the latest professional unit equipped with GPS - the type he was asked to deliver by Comandante Tainted. The unit itself was hard to get because it was manufactured in the USA. Its large and heavy, handheld trunk with coils, two screens, and headphones with a speaker were waterproofed. To be brought to Cuba, this equipment had to be imported initially to Italy from Texas, USA. He, Geovanni, personally traveled to Texas to purchase it and get trained in its use. He will be operating it personally. The faces of Cuban scientists were lighted with enthusiasm.

"*Ahora si!* This is what we need," said Armando. "GPS should be extremely helpful. As you probably know, older models of detectors we were using could not locate the treasure consisting of gold, silver, and precious stones. Also, consider the karst rock of Guanahacabibes is the product of long-term erosion and pressure of water, which converted the rock of the peninsula, you may say, into the karstic mesh. We have over 300 caverns and cave networks crisscrossing this peninsula from coast to coast. This contributed to the disorientation and the difficulties of locating the searchers underground. Gaspar gave us hope that you Geovanni could also help us with the original drawing or some other documentation indicating the cave position. Would this be possible?"

"'*Estimados S-res'*," answered Geovanni, "I don't want to disappoint you neither about the magical abilities of this metal detector, nor about the precision of the map with the location of the treasure we will be searching. Even the latest models of metal detectors can't satisfy all of our requirements. Gold and silver have metallic and mineral properties. This is why the metal detectors should be specifically constructed and calibrated for gold and silver hunting. Happy to explain how they function."

"Metal detectors work by transmitting an electromagnetic field (eddy currents) into the ground," he continued lecturing, "and analyzing the return signal. It is done through its copper coils. Our model has the largest commercially available size of both transmission and receiver coils. Gold detectors take this process a step further by measuring inductance (power of eddy currents) and conductivity (how fast these currents flow), but the size, shape, and presence of minerals in the soil will greatly affect the accuracy of the detector. To remedy this problem, our detector is transmitting the high-frequency signal, not its power. The disadvantage is that this high-frequency signal can penetrate only a shallow depth of the ground, and the high salt content in the ground, which will probably be our case, will produce an error," explained Geovanni.

I observed the long faces of our Cuban hosts. Their enthusiasm cooled down. They were mute processing this new information, which just spoiled their state of resolute security and happiness brought by the initial introduction of new equipment.

"And what about the original documents and drawing of the cave location?" asked Alejandro displaying some disappointment.

"Why were we summoned here instead of the coast between Cabo Frances y Corrientes, where everyone else believed is the location of the cave with treasures? Even Antonio Nunez Jimenez, himself, mentioned that in his book," said Paco.

"If we were to search between Cabo Frances and Corrientes, we could rent rooms in Manuel Lazo. We would have more comfortable accommodations with the water and electricity," growled Armando.

"It is important for the signal of GPS," added Paco, "we would not depend on the limited battery."

"True, why are we planning to search in the middle of nowhere?" wondered Armando. "All previous search expeditions were conducted on the South coast between Cabo Frances y Cabo Corrientes."

"*Compañeros*, those expeditions didn't find the treasure. We would be happy to book you in any lodging for Cubans nearby on Cabo de San Antonio, but there are none. The only hotel in the whole peninsula is in Maria La Gorda, and it is exclusively for hard currency foreigners. We need you here for this search because we have some documents indicating the cave where the cargo from Galleon Princesa de Toledo was stored. It is in the cave of the north-western coast, apparently in the region, which today we call *Los Morros* (Graves), answered Gaspar. "I can´t provide you with more details for now, but we obtained the copy of the friar's alleged testimony and drawing of the location of this cave."

"Fantastic, better than I expected," reacted Paco with visible relief. "This is very important, and for this reason, I am personally willing to camp here. We shall start our search straight away with the appropriate modern metal detector. Now we understand why you insisted on starting with the search here."

"*Gracias*, Doctor. You are right; still, it is not simple. These drawings appear a bit contradictory to our modern eye. When you analyze them, you might notice some discrepancies, maybe because they were made two hundred fifty-five years ago, or maybe because different people drafted them," answered Gaspar.

"We would like to see and analyze these documents before discussing our search plan. We need to confirm their authenticity and precision, please," insisted Paco.

"Meanwhile, since you will have to depart shortly back to your hotel in Maria La Gorda, we were asked to describe for you the specifics of this coast and its caves; it will help our discussion tomorrow to develop a plan for the search," suggested Armando. "Geologically, the whole of Guanahacabibes is a very complex recently formed area. It has nothing in common with the rest of Cuba. We know the limestone substrate of this territory has developed in a very intense process of karstification and an underground water river network," said Armando, "resulting in the relief of naked Carso, its high cracking, high cavernosity, the predominance of *seboruco*, *casimbas* (senotes), holes, sinkholes, grottoes, - all due to the northern coast of Guanahacabibes being a submerged plain of marine origin, with neotectonics tilting of four to six degrees, mainly to the north, resulting in formations of mangroves and swamps.

"According to Dr. Nunes Gimenez in his famous work *Bojeo de Cuba* (Navigating around the coast of Cuba)*,* the Banco de San Antonio is the submerged part of the Guaniguanico mountain range. This underwater mountain being the last peak of the sunken part of Cordillera de Guaniguanico is actually attached to the peninsula. The depth at the Banco de San Antonio drops down one thousand two hundred thirty-five meters to the ocean floor. These flat-topped mountains rising from the deep-sea beds were originally volcanoes. The summit of this sea mountain was eroded in the form of a submarine plateau."

"This land of inhospitable coasts was the last refuge of Cuban aboriginal people fleeing the conquerors," said Paco. "Before the arrival of European man, it was populated by the most primitive and ancient original inhabitants of Cuba, who lived in some of those caves. There could be found valuable cave petrographs and some of their tools. Their activity was restricted to food collection, fishing, hunting."

"Yes, this peninsula is fascinating," said Armando," let me also mention that most coastal caves have a history of serious corrosive action produced by the underground rivers and streams mixing with the tidal sea waters during the storms. The mixing of water is also characteristic in coastal and underwater areas, where marine waters with high concentrations of salts mix with brackish and fresh waters from the sub-horizontal underground flow from karst aquifers. This mixing occurs to a large extent on the coasts due to the ebb and flow of the tide, which introduces marine waters inland at high tide and enhances the flow of freshwater to the sea at low tide. That is why there are so many caverns at the foot of the coastal cliffs and on the walls of the emerged terraces."

"Mario and Arturo are equipped to dive in the subterranean rivers and lakes. They will be helping us to locate the objects we are searching for, if necessary, in submerged areas of the cave. Please leave us the documents you have, compañeros. We will be expecting your return from Maria La Gorda early tomorrow morning, and don't forget to come with all your batteries fully charged," said Alejandro.

Chapter 17

I can't eat this spaghetti with tomato sauce because I am allergic to it; it stinks of garlic and many other hot spices but has no meat. This food is not good for dogs. Mommy Dora always said that tomato sauce and garlic are toxic for dogs. It tasted awful, smelling disgusting, and I refused it.

I knew it! Diego's fault. Why didn't he register me as a foreign dog in La Bajada? I am not used to the kind of food most Cuban people feed their dogs - rice without meat. By the way, I hate and wouldn't touch the stinking, rotten soy mincemeat sold to Cubans on their ration cards. I am not stupid; it is awful. My poor Cuban brothers, I sympathize with your destiny, but this is not my cup of tea.

After Geovanni and Gaspar left, Diego went to see Alejandro and his diver crew in their tent. When Diego returned with puzzled looks to the campfire where we were seated, Armando asked, "What Alejandro said?"

"He said that there are no meat rations for Benz because only humans have the food rations. He became annoyed with me when I insisted on reminding him that Comandante Tainted assured him of good treatment for the dog. Alejandro replied that I should stop this counter-revolutionary talk. When I protested, saying that Benz is a revolutionary dog because he is a working dog, he dismissed me, suggesting that instead of wasting time, I should let Benz kill his food by hunting for wild hugs or hutias (a large, twenty to sixty centimeters long Caribbean rodent) in the forest behind the camp."

"Diego, don't look for troubles. What is new about Alejandro? We don't argue with him. If he wants to control the meat, he will, and all we have to do is let it be, smarten up, *'hermano'* (brother). We must eat our *'hama'* (grub or sustenance), whatever we get, and concentrate tonight on studying the sketches with notes left to us by Gaspar. Meanwhile, why don't you and your dog hunt for wild hugs or anything else, except the turtles, please? It is illegal to hunt turtles. Sorry to say, but many do. Unfortunately, they get away with it. A real crime because many of their species are already on the edge of extinction," warned Paco.

"You are right, brother. There is nothing else left for Benz but to hunt. Which local wild animals are permitted to hunt here and where?" agreed Diego.

"Bueno, the name of the peninsula by itself, answers your question. Many iguanas, crocodiles, wild bores, giant hutias, honey sliders, different types of serpents, and thousands of bats in caverns. Hunt for them in this forest behind us but stay clear of turtles on the beach and flamingoes in coastal mangroves. Only the reptiles are in the swamp and mangrove forest," said Paco.

"The hardwood forest looks slim and fragile because they grow in bare limestone karst consisting of shells and marine fossils with no soil, or, at very best, a skeletal soil derived from limestone and hollow stone," said Armando, "their hard and resistant trunks are slim but very dense. They are valuable for cabinet making, and because of that, they are cut indiscriminately. Their leaves are consumed by the hutia conga or by only recently introduced deer as a target for the paying hard currency foreign hunters. These are good prey for Benz, and maybe he will share with us his kills."

"No *compañeros*, we don't have rifles, nor we will pay the hard currency to kill the dear," said Diego, "but the hutia conga sounds good. We only need the real meat for Benz. As for myself, I survived on this awful, stinky soy mincemeat for the last 25 years, and not because I am a vegetarian."

Diego does not like to kill. He never before let me kill, I thought, *but now he understands that I have no choice: either I kill, or I will starve. I am ready, but I have never done that before, and I hope it will be easy.*

"We shall go hunting in the forest, Diego. I will let my instinct guide me," I barked and pulled on a leash held by Diego.

"Wait, Benz," he resisted, "you devil, stop pulling on me. Let me have my spaghetti first, or it will get cold. We will hunt together. I can't let you go on your own."

While waiting beside Diego until he finished his spaghetti, I brooded about the unfair discrimination against Cuban dogs; *I am already quite hungry. Why are Alejandro and his divers distributing the food? Why not Comandante Tainted, who sent us on this expedition? Probably because I am not a foreign dog but a Cuban, otherwise I would stay with Geovanni and Gaspar in Maria La Gorda to continue eating delicious restaurant-cooked meat dishes. Being a Cuban dog, I am forced to kill to eat. Killing sounds easy, but I am not so certain until I try. Diego is right; we must try hunting the rodents first. I saw the neighbor's cat catching a rodent before. It means I must start by using the tactics of cats.*

We left at dusk for the fragile but dense green cedar forest extending behind the camp. I picked up a recent scent of a large mammal only fifteen or twenty minutes after entering the forest. Of course, what else will you expect from the hungry dog! I pulled Diego hard, trotting with my nose on the ground while following this scent. The seashells and the fossils of marine creatures mixed with some petrified vegetation are forming the ground of this forest. They are loose, not yet bonded, and compacted by time but unstable. The ground springs and rolls under my paws and Diego's feet making it hard for us to run. Diego was unable to keep with me and dropped my leash.

I became ecstatic about the very promising scent of the recently passing large and tasty animal I discovered. My nose was still stuck in a trail when suddenly I run into a huge, black, wild boar. It was the first time in my life that I met a monster like that, at least twice my size but overly broad in shoulders and fat. He was only a couple of feet away from me. What a scare! His vicious little eyes hidden in his large head with a huge mouth and big teeth reflected his bestial anger at being disturbed. His huge white tasks contrasting with his wiry black hair pointed at me with menace. I barked loudly, hoping to scare him, but instead, he charged against me.

I had to retreat and attempt to run away, for there was no chance that I could, on my own, fight such a large, ferocious animal with these huge tusks. I don't have any experience in fighting; how could I be expected to kill! The boar will be the one who will kill, and the dead animal will be me. Diego heard my cry and the noise of the boar running after me. He joined me in running away, shouting my name but tripped in a rolling deposit of shells and fossils on the ground and fell. It made me stop and look back. The boar was gone. I returned to find Diego, who had already gotten up and was now looking for me.

"Forget it, Benz, we haven't trained you before to hunt, and you can't start hunting a large wild boar on your own. I was not given any firearms either. You will do better stalking smaller animals, like the local giant hutia conga, for a start. Better hurry, or soon it will be dark, and we will have to return to our camp without filling your tummy," he warned me.

This time I acted less ambitious, looking for the trucks of small animals while staying as close as possible to the camp. Yes, there were some, and I rushed frantically about, turning, and twisting my course, with my nose again down to the ground, whining as I frantically rushed, leaping abruptly at right angles, reading the full report that many creatures had written on the ground. Finally, I stalked the forest hutia, and when I was close, I felt some noise from above. The hutia climbed the tree trunk to safety. Instead of jumping and barking up to the tree, I hit and waited in my cover of leaves and shadows, staying crouched to the ground, almost on my belly. I waited in this position until hutia was reassured that there was no danger and came down to the ground again. I leaped and stroked hutia as a lightning bolt. He was killed instantly in my jaws when I pierced his throat with my teeth, and his warm blood filled my mouth. It tasted good, but I was not used to the uncooked meat of hutia. Still, the euphoria of accomplishing my first kill for food brought my level of excitement beyond control. I was spinning around madly shaking my prey.

When Diego arrived, I came straight to him, holding in my jaws the bleeding dead pray, nearly 60 cm long, and proudly put it on the ground in front of him. Diego was extremely impressed. He pronounced a speech of pride for me as a hunter, attached the dead hutia to a stick, and we returned to the camp before the darkness swallowed us up. Everyone in the camp came to see my kill. They were all praising me, but the kill was mine, and I have already given it to Diego. Now it should be his decision who will eat my kill. Juan skinned and cleaned the body of hutia, then barbequed it on spits over the campfire. It was all given to me, and it was super delicious.

I was full, satisfied, and felt very proud of myself. When the scientists left to sleep inside their tents, I stayed with the guard (the navy divers took turns to guard the fire) beside the fire thinking that adversity actually is very good for dogs, and maybe even for men.

If Alejandro would not refuse my food rations, I reflected, *I would never learn that I can be a great hunter, capable of providing Diego and myself with wild meat every day if we would need to hunt for our food in the forest.*

The silence was broken by the concert of the forest animals and the beating of the branches. It was a cool night with a very pleasant sea breeze, and despite all excitement and a strong smell of burned guava and arabo tree sticks, I fell asleep until the morning breeze. In the early morning, Alejandro with his divers joined us for morning coffee. As always, dismissive of me and my talents, he said he was not surprised that I could kill hutia but not the boar.

"Dobermans," he said, "have not been used as hunting dogs, only as of the chasers of Jews and slaves. They can track the scent of *cimarrones* (escaped slaves) from far away. That is because the Jews and blacks have a special scent."

He always repeats this nonsense. How would Doberman know who are Jews and slaves and who are not? Each human has a unique scent of his own, just like every dog. Each scent is due to the type of food they eat and the state of their health, basically reflecting the environmental odors of the individual and not on his religion or skin color.

Juan, the forester, neither could take these stupidities any longer and defended me by saying that one dog is simply not enough; it is necessary to use a pack of three or four dogs, and the hunter shall have a gun. If Diego had a gun, he could shoot the boar. Diego said, "I am happy with the kill of hutia. It is sufficient meat for Benz, and I would not allow Benz to risk the battle with a larger pray without the support of firearms."

"In such a case," said Alejandro, "I might be coming with you in the future to hunt a boar or a dear with my Kalashnikov. It must be fun and will provide all of us with sufficient meat. Where is the last night meat of hutia?"

"Benz ate it last night, and I was told that his main task is not providing us with food here but searching for the gold and silver," answered Diego.

He does not know where I hid the bones with meat last night inside the forest, I thought, *or he might be afraid that Alejandro will steal my bones. I better hide them deeper and cover the ground with branches.*

At this moment, the car with Geovanni and Gaspar arrived. After hearing the report about my heroic kill and praising me for it, they sat down at the table drinking coffee to discuss the documents left with the scientists last night. I decided that it was urgent for me, while they were distracted, to make sure that nobody could find my hutia bones loaded with meat and juicy collagen. When they set around the sketches on the table and started arguing, I slipped away into the forest where I hit what was left of hutia last night. After its unearthing, I had a few good bites of meat and dug a new deeper hole, where I deposited my treasure, filled the hole with shells and sand, and covered it with the tree branches. When I returned to the camp, the members of the expedition were still discussing maps. They even didn't notice my absence.

"All you said is true; I would like to point out that the map of the cave and its description left with us last night looks sufficiently authentic in the old Spanish language of the period. Naturally, there is no GPS location of the cave itself; this was not possible in the XVII century, but it gives us approximate distances to the points of reference. It details how the cargo with barrels and clay jars was transferred during the night from the beach to the cave, how the priests and marine crew found the mouth of the cave in the forest near the beach, surrounded by *'dientes del perro'* and pockets of mangrove. The distances from the cave to the reference points shall help us to locate the cave of interest despite the abundance of sand and cave pockets in the Cabo de San Antonio," said Paco. "Only a few of these hidden caves were visited and properly examined until today. With the modern tools, we will be able to do a better job."

Suddenly, I felt a scent of a dog and a human approaching our camp. I stood up and sniffed the air in the direction this scent emerged. Indeed, the scent was getting stronger in the direction of the forest, and I started barking to alarm Diego and the others in our pack that the strangers were coming. Initially, all humans were complaining that I was out of control, interfering with their discussions until an unknown middle-aged, black man dressed as a farmer man appeared from the forest holding a nice-smelling, good-looking, young female of mixed breed, cream-colored, skinny dog on the leash. I stood back not only because Diego called on me but because no respectable male dog should attack a female. We dogs are not like humans, my instinct would not allow me to be rude to a female dog, so I sat down.

Juan was very happy to see this man and introduced him as his friend and partner for patrolling the coast forester. His name is Pipo; like Diego, he is a Cuban ex-soldier who returned from Angola. The name of the young and beautiful, very short fur, blond bitch, who immediately took an interest in me, is Rubia. Juan and Pipo, with their dog, were to patrol on their feet the forty kilometers of the coast. The command post of rangers was located only four kilometers from La Barca; it is exceptionally poorly powered by the experimental solar panels but has a phone and a small refrigerator to keep their drinking water cold. Pipo was married and had two children; basically, being a farmer, he was working very hard as a forester to provide food for his family.

After new greetings and introductions, our humans sat down at the table to drink their coffee. Pipo and Juan described the complexities of their job, consisting of catching illegal activities on the peninsula, such as logging, illegal hunting, and most dangerous of all, illegal drugs. Packs of drugs wrapped in nylon are thrown offshore by traffickers arriving from Yucatan at the San Antonio coast when swept away by sea currents to these shores. They were right; in addition to the Chief Justice of the National

Revolutionary Police Sector in the area, an agent from the Anti-Drug Department of the Ministry of the Interior arrived half an hour later. It was his job to verify every person in the area and warn that none of these packages found on the beach should be open. Instead, the packages must be put aside, and the police must be notified.

This is why the rangers need Rubia, I thought. *Surely Rubia would know all local scents and would locate for rangers the illegal activities.* The rangers take all credit for catching them by themselves, but I understand and feel great admiration for the beautiful and intelligent Rubia. She is a natural tracking working dog.

The rangers were complaining about the difficulties of their job due to walking on their feet in the mix of tangled thorns and *'dientes de perro'*, in overgrown coastal mangrove and cedar karst forest. My thoughts were about Rubia: *how hard it is for her small, bare paws.*

"Our scientists just described to us how difficult it would be searching in this area. You must help us, *compañieros,*" said Gaspar. "We are looking for a coastal cave in Cabo de San Antonio, which is drawn in this sketch. It is confusing because the priest who made this sketch was not local and had no knowledge of cartography. He was not aware and couldn't name the coastal points for reference."

"You probably looking, same as the Comandante Tainted recently did, for the famous Treasures of Merida," said Pipo. "There are some coastal caves on the northern coast of this peninsula fitting your sketch. A few larger caves close to the lighthouse and on the peninsula's southern coast were visited and given names. There are dozens of smaller ones, which were not. The greatest problem is the difficult access to the caves on the northern coast of Cabo de San Antonio because of dense mangroves overgrowing the coastal *'diente de perro'.*"

Chapter 18

My attention got distracted by the incomprehensible, wonderful scent emanating from Rubia. Her scent completely overtook me, and, of course, I could resist neither her gorgeous looks nor her graceful gait. She is a lively and beautiful girl of medium-large size but smaller than me with a long snout, large erect ears, bright eyes shining like topaz, and long eyelashes. Her short cream-blond fur is shiny, and her long tail is welcoming my approach, but what made her absolutely irresistible was the fantastic, pungent smell that made me understand how she felt. She went in heat, but me - I simply lost my mind. The call of nature is stronger than the chains of human dogma.

We forgot about our humans and started gently smelling each other scents. I knew I fell in love. We just met, but she was already sniffing under my tail. My heartbeat quickened. I gently shifted her backside. O, heavens! Her delightful pungent fragrance, very strong and totally new to me, smelled fantastic and made me very excited. I had never before smelled anything so wonderful in my life. Rubia was sniffing my paws at length, and she made me forget my chastity vows. I felt like giving my life for running away together with this beauty.

When I asked her if she would like to eat the rest of my barbequed hutia, which I hit under the forest ground, she consented. We took advantage of humans being busy and run together side by side, away from them into the shadow of the forest. I even forgot about *'jijenes'* and mosquitos attacking us as soon as we left the campfire with the guava and arabo tree sticks. Our instinct and affection for each other completely overtook us.

When we finally hid in the forest, we run at each other, went up on our back legs, clashed our heads, fell on the ground, and roll about on its sandy soil mixed with shells. I knew that it meant I was accepted as her boyfriend. I rubbed my snout against her neck, meaning that I was ready to do all it takes. I would provide the food for her for the rest of our lives. But Rubia is an alfa-female, so she does not roll on her back, she started laughing and said that this was a nice romantic gesture, but a city dog could hardly aspire to become an efficient provider for her in a forest.

Still, she was impressed with my gentlemen's looks and my smarts, indicating that she was willing to love me with passion. She stood firm on her four paws and coyly moved her tail aside, inviting me to jump her. This time my instincts took over, and I forgot all my previous reasons, including my responsibilities in the expedition. Our natural instinct just took over and guided our first sex experience, which was more than we could ever enjoy in paradise. It felt as if we had traveled into cosmic space and back when lying on the ground, still locked together, recovering from separation, when we heard the voices of Diego and Pipo calling our names. How inconsiderate, these humans feel entitled to spoil the intimate moments of their pets any time they are pleased. What a shame!

When Diego and Pipo found us, they understood our situation and our reluctance to return with them back to the camp. They took us before our joining with the rest of the members of the expedition for a dip on the beach made of very fine silica white sand and warm emerald-green water. How beautiful was Rubia in my eyes when she appeared crowned by the rainbow from shaking her fur under the morning sun! *There is nobody like her in the whole creation. I want to marry her and have with her many babies,* I thought. I looked at Diego, and he was not angry, but rather happy for me.

"Diego," I asked when Pipo and Rubia couldn't hear me, "maybe Geovanni will understand my feelings and forgive me for breaking the celibacy vows of the Catholic church. I want to marry Rubia."

"Don't tell this to me and don't talk about it to anyone else, my friend," answered Diego. "Don't you worry about the priests of the Catholic church. They break these vows by themselves quite often. All we have to do is to find the treasure, and all our sins will be forgotten."

"Forgotten sins are not sufficient, Diego. I still want to marry Rubia and raise the children with her. Could I do that?" I asked.

"I see, Sr. Romeo, you are in love. We will have to discuss it with Pipo and your adoptive parents. You will need to ask them for their blessing, except we will discuss it later; we have other priorities right now. What we need to discuss now is a plan for search in caves."

I agreed, "I will help you, Diego, and you must help me."

Everybody was looking at us with curiosity when we approached, Rubia and me side by side. I noticed that some team members were emanating with understanding and compassion, except Alejandro, who met us with contempt, "Are you already screwing around, the troublemakers? If we wouldn't need you to scare the bats, I would better tie you down here in camp to guard our possessions while we are searching in the caves."

"Our team is waiting for you, Diego and Pipo," explained Gaspar trying to calm down Alejandro, "dogs are important for our cave search; they will take the lead inside the cavern. Most of the caves are home to millions of bats. They might attack us from the ceilings and walls of the caves if they are disturbed. They are dangerous because their bites may be infected. Bats emit ultrasonic pulses of great intensity, measuring over a hundred decibels in the frequency range of thirty to hundred twenty kilohertz.

Humans can not hear sounds greater than eighty decibels and only in frequencies between twenty Hertz and twenty kilohertz, but dogs can hear sounds in frequencies from sixty-seven hertz to forty-five kilohertz. This is why dogs can detect bats, and bats know that dogs will kill them, so they stay away."

How interesting! I didn't know why it was that I could hear bats and humans not. Finally, some recognition, but what about my detection and location of electronic bags in a state visitor's house? I thought. *Why wasn't I recognized on that occasion?*

"The bat produces a sound with its larynx and modifies it with the strange shapes of its nose and mouth," continued Gaspar, "The echoes return and change the sound of vibrations in their inner ear, reporting the echoes received to their brain. Incredibly, this is the same basic principle of radar. Using the echo generated by ultrasound, they can perceive and obtain vital information about their environment, especially about their prey. In the echo, they encode information about the distance to their prey, thanks to the delay between the emitted signal and the reception of the echo. They can also calculate their target speed, size, texture, and location."

"Enough of talking," said Alejandro. "I want to see all your equipment, cave gear, and uniforms. Everyone should pile it up in front of them before our lunch. Nobody will be allowed to carry anything I haven't seen."

While Alejandro was looking at the metal detector, its batteries, the clinometer and notebooks for mapping, the light sources, the led lamps, spares, the machetes, the heavy boots, the overalls, the helmets with chin straps for each team member, and the canisters with ore for me, Rubia and I positioned ourselves beside Gerardo, who took advantage of Alejandro being busy to share with us the meat patties brought by him and Geovanni from hotel in Maria La Gorda, where they stayed overnight. I was glad they have because, in our romantic passion, we forgot about the hutia I hit, and now we felt very hungry. After our breakfast, Rubia and I complained about the lack of privacy, thanks to Alejandro, who ordered us to tie down on the long leash in the camp center. Still, everybody being busy with the preparations, ignored our complaints.

As soon as the humans finished their lunch, Diego and Pipo untied our leashes to join a forming group of expeditors at the front. The rest of the humans, except Juan, who stayed behind to guard the camp and cook the meal, were carrying the cave paraphernalia on their shoulders. Pipo ordered Rubia to proceed toward the coastal keys being a reference point on our map, and I run beside my beloved with our noses to the ground and our humans behind us on the leash. Rubia is a great asset to me because she knows all odors, scents, and fragrances of this forest and all its animals and plants. She was sharing her knowledge with me, but my mind and nose were still overtaken by her wonderful scent. When mosquitos again attacked us in the forest, she said that I need to switch off my mind from their bites, and my immunity will kick in, preventing me from the nervous reaction and suffering when they bite. She said what is really important for me was to learn the scent of snakes and crocodiles from the coastal mangroves. These could be deadly! Thanks, at least one of us was awake, I am ashamed to say, but all these reptiles were totally new to my diet.

"You need to recognize the scent of gigantic green marine turtles, who arrive to lay their eggs in the sand, and the scent of iguanas to protect them and their eggs from anyone who will try to steal them. Many local people used to do just that, and it is our job to find and prevent them," she said. "The wild bores and giant hutias are our fair pray, and humans will be grateful to us if we help to kill them. The wild turkeys and dear are very rare in these areas, and we will have to walk a long time to the East if we wish to hunt them. Huge snails and shells are everywhere, but only humans collect them to eat; we dogs can't get them out from their shells."

Teaching me the local smarts and smells while trotting with our noses in the ground following the scent, Rubia brought us near the beach area where the coral keys were connecting with the coast. This was a different world of intermixed sand and mangroves. Bright-green coastal vegetation suddenly gave way, revealing the marshland lurking below.

Dog's weight is much better distributed than the weight of humans for such terrain, and our four soft paws have the advantage of greater agility compared with the heavy boots of our two-legged humans. Light and blessed with speed, power, and a fine sense of balance, we dogs can shift their body weight in this treacherous terrain and avoid getting trapped. Our humans were now left quite back, and they allowed our leashes free.

I was the first to arrive at the coast and came head-to-head with a massive, reminding a huge wooden trunk, an ugly beast that was completely blocking our way. It was most likely sunning itself on a narrow stretch of coastal sand. If I knew what it was, I would allow myself to back away gracefully, but I didn't. Rubia barked from behind, ordering me to retreat, but how could I show my girlfriend that I was a coward? Instead, I went for it as if this beast would be a snake.

Unfortunately, this was not a snake. Still, being taken by surprise, I behaved like an idiot. Barking furiously and dashing from side to side, ducking low, then dancing ahead as if to strike, I confronted this beast. Rubia joined me in hysterical barking, seeing that I was not retreating; she positioned herself beside me.

The crocodile sat there unmoving, seemingly asleep but watching us from behind slitted eyes. As Rubia came closer, my confidence got the better of me. At that very moment, the crocodile struck. Moving with lightning speed, propelling his large body forwards, his jaws opening and showing the rows of huge teeth slicing down across each other. I jumped ahead to protect Rubia from the crocodile and knocked her backward. The flashing maw missed us by inches when we finally heard the shouts from behind us. These were our humans who saved us from the crocodile. Hearing our incessant, hysterical barking, our humans rushed to the battlefield, yelling abuse at the crocodile, and shooting their guns in the air. Hearing the gunshot and sensing danger, the crocodile thrashed its tail a few times and wriggled back into the water.

Still shocked, Rubia and I sniffed each other in our best possible attempt to examine for any damage and luckily were reassured in being shaken but intact. Meanwhile, the other humans were busy measuring four hundred-forty Spanish varas from the coastal coral keys, the small estuary of the river, and the forest, given in an old sketch from the Vatican. Rubia and I investigated the area for the possible presence of other crocodiles and serpents. Having been reassured of our safety, we proceeded to sniff the site for other creatures, which are abundant but not threatening: crabs, snails, and spiders.

When our humans finally called us to proceed in the direction they had chosen, we had already recuperated from the battle with the crocodile. We proceeded towards the low forest, where unexpectantly, after a while, we bumped into a cave mouth surfacing from the karst floor.

The entrance was of medium height, good for dogs but low for humans. They would have to bend at its entrance. The cave mouth was difficult to notice, for it is covered with *la uva caleta* (linguee) overgrow. My heart was filled with even more admiration for the nose of Rubia because I realized that without her, we probably would not find this cave. The compass of our humans who followed us went utterly bizarre, with its needle turning nonstop as soon as we came near the cave.

After our eyes got used to the dim lights of a large interior hall of a cave carved in naked limestone, Rubia and I began walking along its walls, reading the scents of its residents who could present a danger, such as snakes, bats, and spiders. There was some offensive scent, but before we could find the threat, we discovered an opening of a tunnel into which we proceeded illuminated with the lights of Diego's and Pipo's helmets. It led us into a still larger hall with a higher ceiling, resembling a gigantic dome. The rest of the humans followed us.

This salon was quite impressive with tall columns and stalactites; I wanted to start its investigation but was told to wait for everybody else to join us and start using the bigger lights. To our surprise, this large hall resembling a gigantic dome with columns, stalagmites, and stalactites contained a large nasty-looking and nasty-smelling, very dark, almost black lake in the center of the hall. The scientists measured it as large as ninety-two meters by fifty-seven meters and approximately ten meters deep at its shore. We didn't know how deep it was at the center.

"Amazing crystal sculptures, I heard of these before; how do they form under the ground?" asked Geovanni.

"This is a phreatic cave," answered Armando. "Its karst is cracked, and rainwater seeps through. It passes through organic material, and picks up carbon dioxide gas, creating carbonic acid, which dissolves the limestone rock, now exposed to the air in the cave. It releases carbon dioxide gas, causing the precipitation of calcite on cave walls, ceilings, and floors. As the redeposited minerals build up, a stalactite is formed. Stalactites grow down from the cave ceiling, while stalagmites grow up from cave the cave floor."

"Thank you for a good explanation, and how such a large lake could have been formed under the ground?" asked Geovanni.

"The terrestrial rivers in Guanahacabibes are running under the *'diente del perro'* (coastal *seboruco*), said

Armando. "They emerge in the mountains and find their way to the sea, moving through long cracks and spelts of the Isthmus, until they deposit into the sea or collect as lakes in large underground depressions, like this one."

Our humans were worried about their compasses being still not functional. The same happened to Geovanni when he attempted to start his metal detector. The needle of his instrument was also turning around in chaos.

"This is why the whole San Antonio area is called '*sorda*' (deaf) - meaning no radio and electromagnetic signals could be detected there," commented Paco. "Look at the marine navigational maps, and you will see that the marine channel running parallel to the whole coast of Cabo de San Antonio is called *Paso Sorda del Muerto*. (Deaf Channel of Dead). A pretty nasty name and nobody knows why. We suspect there are uranium deposits somewhere in the area."

Rubia and I were less concerned about lost magnetic signals. We went around the dark lake in the center and noticed the slight movement of water downstream where it possibly was discharging at a distance into the underground river on the lower level. The weird formations on walls, ceiling, and floor, shaped it into unimaginable forms, some like draped and others like rock flowers.

"It is magic! Nature is a true artist creating imaginative structures like these, apparently made of crystal," marveled Geovanni.

"No, not of crystal; it is made of limestone. Limestone is usually a biological sedimentary rock, forming from the accumulation of shell, coral, algal, fecal, and other organic debris. It can also form by chemical sedimentary processes, such as the precipitation of calcium carbonate from lake or ocean water," said Armando.

Rubia and I put out noses to the floor around the walls of this salon. As I moved to the back wall, the heat, and the strange stench coming from somewhere inside one of connecting tunnels, unpleasantly surprised me.

"What the hell is all that smell?" I asked Rubia.

"It is the scent of bats," she said. I know that for sure. It smells as if they are in very large numbers somewhere at a distance," she said.

I looked up and noticed some bats on the ceiling, but my nose, when I sniffed the air to determine the direction from which the stench was coming, led me to the dark tunnel opening on the side of the back wall. It was slightly ascending. Near this ascending wider tunnel opening, Rubia found another, even more, narrow passageway slightly descending apparently to a lower level. I launched into the offensively smelling, ascending tunnel to find the possible threat to our team and us. Diego called me back to wait for him until he could catch up with me and light my way. I righteously disobeyed; *what if someone dangerous is stalking us?*

I don't need the lights the way humans do. I have natural night vision, and my snout receives more information than my eyes. Rubia was reluctant to follow me. I knew that I should not allow a female to become the first scout to protect me from a possible danger expecting us in the unknown. Protection is my job. Diego, busy with removing the ore can from his backpack, gave up when I answered that I couldn't wait to start the search of the stinky backroom. I dragged Diego on my leash through the passageway for what seemed to be a long time until we came to a really hot large room. The temperature in this room was worst than any Cuban hot temperatures I ever experienced before. Rubia, with Pipo on her leash, was behind us. There also was a very high humidity of the air, close to the saturation point.

"'*Ojo*'" (Watch it)," said Pipo. "This could be a hot room. Bats are the main source of this heat. The first thing when you are close to their room is the increase in temperature and arthropods on its walls and floors and ceil (beetles, moisture insects, mites, spiders, cockroaches, and polylas)."

As soon as we entered this room, we felt choking with the hot air and an incredible guano stench. Horrendous chaos was produced by the thousands of bats that were disturbed by our lights. The recirculation of hot air in the cave enclosure was limited to the highest degree because of the restricted connections with the outside. It was penetrating our airways as if it was burning. The rest of the human team following us behind were now blocking the entrance preventing our escape from this hell. The loud flapping broke the silence of the cave of the thousands of bats, which, frightened by the light of the lanterns and the human presence, were attempting to leave the room all at once.

"Such a room is called a thermal trap in the exchange zone. It can be conditioned by an abrupt narrowing of the room or by a change in level or its direction," said Armando.

"Look at the ground," Rubia warned me. "Mites on the ground. Don't touch them, they are parasites, or you will get very sick."

"You see a real living carpet on the floor," said Paco, "made up of hundreds of thousands of mites, mostly parasites of bats."

"We locals call these rooms '*salas de infierno*' (halls of hell)," said Pipo.

The people behind us were choking with stench and pushed back towards the exit in an attempt to protect their burning airways, crashing with curious and anxious military divers caring for the equipment in the back of the procession.

"Why and how the hell like this was created?" asked Geovanni.

"The caloric energy released from the bodies of thousands of bats usually crowded into a small cave space where the air is barely renewed. It is coupled with the loss of water due to perspiration and urination by the bats themselves, plus the heat generated by the fermentation of guano, which determines that such a climate produces a very stable microclimate where the temperature and the humidity approach the saturation point. These conditions are created by bats, and without them, there would be no heat caves," explained Paco.

"We must leave this room immediately, or we will get sick," grunted Pipo.

"Indeed, poor air circulation in a restricted cave covered with fermented guano and urine of bats produces the concentration of ammonia; it may cause severe injury and eye burns," said Paco.

Right, Rubia and I have to retreat now, I thought, reacting to this awful strong smell killing my nose. *We must get out from the 'halls of hell' at any cost. If I need, I will push those slow humans blocking the exit.*

Chapter 19

Mommy Dora said that the canine second nose - the olfactory cortex is part of the canine brain; actually, it is thirty-five percent of a dog's brain. It means that any damage to our nose will render us, dogs, mentally challenged or convert us into 'mad as dogs', the name humans often call their own kind. We can't afford that; it will be our death sentence. Our first instinct was to protect our snouts immediately, and I barked to Rubia, begging her to follow me. I must admit, we added to the chaos of our already panicky human friends when we knocked them down to get away from this hellish room and rushed back through the passageway, leaving them to follow us if they can. We stopped only when we reached the mouth of the first entrance room to the outside.

"This your dog has led us straight into hell," angrily growled Alejandro. "Gaspar, you are confused or misinformed. We must review your references and get rid of these mad dogs."

My reputation will be ruined even before I started the sniffing of ore-search in front of my beloved. Not fair; I even haven't finished my initial investigation of all passageways, I thought. I looked at Gaspar, barked a couple of times, and stalked towards the narrow passage slightly inclined below, apparently to a lower level. Diego pointed out to my signal announcing that I took a new lead, and he wanted to follow me into this second narrower tunnel.

"No, it is getting too late; we must return to the camp and continue tomorrow," objected Alejandro.

For the first time since I met him, Alejandro said something I liked. I, too, preferred to get out of this cavern and start hunting with Rubia for our food. I turned around and enthusiastically touched with my nose the nose of Rubia, "Hurrah! We finished the stinking business for today and shall hunt for dinner. I am already hungry; how about you?"

We trotted in unison to the exit from the cave, with humans following us towards the coastal vegetation of the sand dune. The high tide brought patches of yellow and brown *sargasso* into the area, and I noticed a gigantic turtle struggling to overcome this obstacle.

"Rubia, Benz stay," shouted Pipo. "Don't bark or move. We came into a nesting area of green turtles. They can not be disturbed!"

I looked at Rubia; she was transfixed, stalking another turtle, which managed to free herself from the stinking, brown *sargasso*.

"This sargasso increases the number of failed nesting attempts and makes it difficult for turtles to access the beach," said Pipo, "it is also an extra obstacle for newborns on their way to the sea."

"It creates problems not only for turtles. It also affects coastal and reef ecosystems, interfering with photosynthesis and reducing oxygen levels in the water," said Armando.

We all became motionless, observing the turtles. Soon, I noticed another turtle, which has already made her bed – a large and shallow hole, where she will lay her eggs and cover them with sand to protect them from predators. These turtles were huge – as large as my own body in diameter. Diego and Pipo approached calmly and put us on a leash. Then they pulled us away. Pipo said, that he and Juan will have to return here to clear the beach to ensure that sargasso does not prevent the turtles from nesting and their babies from reaching the ocean in forty-five days during the nestling pick.

"I understand," said Geovanni, "that after mothers cover the eggs with the sand, they depart back into the sea. Who will be looking after and protecting their eggs for forty-five days? Are they safe?"

"Unfortunately, not," said Pipo. "Even before their birth, they are already attacked by insect larvae, ants, crabs, wild pigs, or human poachers. The superstition created global markets for them, without any basis, assigned them aphrodisiac properties. After the babies break the eggshell, they will have to dig through more than half a meter of sand to get to the surface. Leaving the nest might take three days or a week. On average, only one in a thousand newborns will reach the reproductive age of sixteen years."

Sounds horrible, I thought. *We dogs are much luckier. Suppose Rubia and I will have the pups. There is a good chance the majority of them will survive. Thankfully, there is no market for dog meat in Cuba yet.*

In the late afternoon, we returned to the camp. Giovanni and Gaspar took off in their car to make it in time for a nice hot shower and dinner in the hotel of Maria La Gorda.

"The presence of Geovanni is no longer required because *'que corajo'* (damn it) his metal detector proved to be useless in this area where the electromagnetic signals are blocked. Geovanni can return tonight to Maria La Gorda and tomorrow to Havana," said Alejandro before they left.

"In my opinion, the other underground passages, which we are planning to investigate tomorrow, might have a different electromagnetic condition," objected Gaspar.

The scientists and rangers supported his opinion, and Alejandro reluctantly calmed down. We, the dogs, were let off the leash to hunt in the surrounding forest. Juan was already cooking '*arroz con frijoles*' (rice with beans) for dinner, but Pipo assured him that we would bring some meat for barbeque, took his rifle, and followed us. He and Diego walked together behind us into the forest, sharing their memories of Angola.

Energized by the happiness of being together and allowed to do what we really like – hunting, gave us second air. I felt very happy, and the temptation to brag in front of my beautiful girl was stronger than my good judgment.

"Yes, I have killed many wild boars. The last one was as tall as a man, and he weighed more than two horses," I barked.

"Which kind of dog are you? Are you a bay dog or a catch dog?" asked Rubia.

"Well, I am a Doberman – gentleman's dog," I answered in confusion. "What the hell is a bay dog or a catch dog? I never met them in Tarara where I am coming from."

"In this case, please just follow me if you don't even know what a bay dog or a catch dog means. Bay dogs harass and harry the boar, keeping it cornered in one place and barking loudly. Catch dogs grip the boar with their jaws, typically seizing the base of the boar's ear. Once they have the boar, they will hold it down by the head until the hunter arrives. And, by the way, we don't hunt for the gentlemen here, only for boars, stags, and hutias."

She figured my lies out; what a shame. I shall give up before too late, I thought.

"Sounds good, darling, never mind the confusion with different types of dogs; I am in love with you and will follow you to the end of Earth, but what kind of dog are you?"

"I can do both," she said and took a stalking pose. I also picked up a scent similar to the one I experienced yesterday with the boar. We put our noses to the ground and trotted into the forest, tracking this scent. Fifteen minutes later, we met with the same wild boar which I was chasing yesterday. We started a loud barking and started a chase after him. When he finally stopped to face us, we prevented him from escaping. Pipo following us behind shot the boar into his head. We were standing close to the boar, and the rifle shot felt very loud and nasty as if my eardrums had exploded. Poor boar got a huge black hole on the front of his head and a minute later was lying dead on the ground with a gaping wound gashing out a massive amount of blood. I was shocked; I guess it is the law of jungles, kill or be killed. Rubia pretended nothing happened and left with Pipo to look for the tree's branches, which were needed to carry the boar carcass.

This time nobody paid attention to me; they were busy draining excess blood and tying the carcass of boar to the large wood branches, then we victoriously carried the dead boar back to the camp. That night Rubia and I had for dinner the boar's shoulder. I must admit it was very delicious. Everyone was very happy with our successful hunting and their barbeque. When they went to sleep, Rubia and I, in the privacy of the forest, once again, found the paradise we were longing for all day. Then after our delicious, heavenly lovemaking, we returned to the camp to lay side by side beside the campfire with the guava tree sticks slow-burning all night. This was my best sleep and the happiest night of my life.

In the early morning, Gaspar and Geovanni returned from their hotel in Maria La Gorda. After breakfast, we departed in the same contingent as yesterday, except for taking with us a delicious lunch with slices of barbequed boar's meat, packed inside the bread and plenty of good fresh water brought by Gaspar from Maria La Gorda. Today, it took us less time to walk towards the same cavern entrance mouth because now we knew where it was. Entering the cavern, Rubia and I sniffed the air – no scent of a stranger was detected. Nobody has been here since we left yesterday. We stood at the entrance of the narrow underground passage leading downwards, and I looked at

Diego and barked, requesting his permission to examine it. This time permission was given, and I went ahead with Diego at my heels, illuminating our way with the lights of his headset. This passage was more difficult to proceed with. Sometimes Diego would slow down because he had to crawl on his knees. Additionally, after a while, I picked the scent of the serpent hiding somewhere farther away. This made me very worried because it would be difficult to fight the serpent if it attacks in such a narrow passageway.

The passageway was leading us in the same direction as yesterday, but it was inclined downwards this time. It took me approximately the same long time as yesterday to arrive at this lower gallery room. I was very careful in moving around while investigating this room because I still could smell the scent of the serpent. Rubia and Pipo came behind us, and she also warned me about the sneak. We discovered a low rock debris pile with colored balls resting on its mineralized surface at the center of the room. Seeing these colored balls, Diego ordered us to investigate the surrounding area but forbid us from touching and biting the colored balls. Giovanni continued struggling with his metal detector again, producing no results but plenty of aggravation. Alejandro observed him with contempt, but his main attention was focused on the colored balls in the center of the room.

When the scientists arrived, they became very excited and picked up the balls of each color to examine them; they asked Alejandro for permission to collect some samples for the laboratory definition of their origins.

"These look like the pearls of the cave," said Armando. "Its origin is due to the long-term successive crystallization around small primitive irritants of calcium carbonate which forms in water paddles where the water dripping continues. The principal ingredient is calcite; in some cases, it could be aragonite. Basically, 'the pearls of the cave' are balls of calcium carbonate. They are hard, similar to these, smooth and shiny: these are the porcelain pearls. These pearls are mostly spherical or egg-shaped."

Alejandro interrupted him with suspicion. "What is about their colors and brill?"

"Color could be white, grey, yellow, or red," said Paco. "They could differ in size: some as small as the head of the needle, others as big as the orange."

"Right, I never heard about pearls of the cave before. No, you can not collect specimens. They must be given to Mario for their safekeeping. This is an order and no more arguments. Have you Pipo seen anything like these before?" asked Alejandro.

"Never before," answered Pipo, "but I heard that in some caverns, the nests with dozens of precious-colored eggs, that brill, might be hidden," mooted Pipo worried about the possible consequences of his admission.

"I don't know about their value," spoke Armando," but I will send you the work of Nunez Jimenez and other international publications about this phenomenon. Actually, they conclude that 'the pears of the cave' are the secondary product of guano. The cave with bats and their guano above this one could be leaking. So, these colored balls are probably 'the pearls of guano'. Meanwhile, we are happy to comply with your orders, whatever you like."

"I repeat: all pearls are to be picked up and given to Mario for keep. We will find out what they are and their value without your international publications," ordered Alejandro.

The scientists stood back, allowing Mario and Arturo to harvest the pearls, which lay freely, not being attached to the underlying surface. They counted over two hundred multicolored pearls and stored them in a bag. Diego held the can with ore to me, and I took a deep sniff of its contents, then attempted to find a similar scent in the air and on the ground of the room. Nothing, my efforts miserably fell.

There was no scent of golden ore that I could smell, only the persistent scent of a serpent. I felt embarrassed, almost like a loser in the same boat as Geovanni. Rubia and Diego looked disappointed but avoided commentaries.

Suddenly a serpent stroked at Mario from behind the pile of balls when he bent down to pick up one. Rubia sprang stiff-legged around the serpent and managed to corner her. For its part, the serpent probably never set eyes before on such an adversary – a dog. I jumped from the side and met the attack of the serpent, which darted its head forward to strike. I sprang in the other direction, also seeking the perfect time to strike it. When this moment came, Rubia and I together darted in lightning-fast, attacking with paws and jaws until the battle was very much won. Then I grabbed the limp form of the serpent of nearly two meters long in my mouth and carried it proudly to the feet of Rubia. It was a noble and beautiful moment.

"What's the hell it is now?" shouted Armando, taken by surprise.

"This is a local serpent '*el maja*' as we call them," said Pipo, "it lives in caves with bats because the fruit bats are their main food. It is possible that this '*maja*' was hunting for lizards or spiders which came from the cave with bats above, and it is also possible that we will find other serpents here as well because they hunt together."

"Send dogs to help Mario and Arturo to collect all the pearls," ordered Alejandro, now worried for his divers.

Ja, now we became important to the military, that's nice. Hope our good luck will continue, I thought, as we stayed on guard beside Mario and Arturo, watching for serpents or large spiders until they finished harvesting colored pearls.

Alejandro, still busy with the supervision of his divers collecting the colored balls, was whispering to himself, "The pearls of guano, I never heard that before."

Dogs know better, I thought, *that the pearls, never mind which, of guano or even of oysters, are not good to eat. They are probably of no use because they don't smell of ore either; therefore, these are not treasures. When in doubt, let's eat; it is lunchtime.*

Chapter 20

On our return to the entrance salon, I told Rubia to join me in asking for some food. We succeeded by nudging our humans who, when feeling uncertain about the next action, as is usual in such cases, decided to eat before discussing the next move. Good idea, finally! Their expectations of miracles by using a new metal detector were frustrated by the absence of magnetic signals. Yes, it was a big downer for them, and they were now apprehensive about failure.

The humans are only interested in golden ore treasure, I thought. *Until they find it, they will continue complaining and will not help our human and canine team in Tarara to get rid of mad Colonel Beltran, who might eat us alive. I must think fast.*

I sniffed the air in the entrance salon attentively. Diego held the open ore can to my nose, helping me to refresh my scent memory. Indeed, now I could feel the slight smell of golden ore scent coming from the lake in the center of the cave. Considering the lake's dark and not inviting water, its depth at the center, and its unknown chemical content, we shied away from it initially. Still, I decided that it was worthwhile to investigate the scent coming from under its water. I barked and stalked at the lake's shore, requesting permission to jump into the water. Rubia did not join me. Either she did not understand why I was stalking it, or she was disgusted by the color and content of its water.

"Don't get wet with this water," she barked. "I don't like swimming. Also, it looks too turbulent and dark, and smells like a strange fish to me."

It is an opportunity for me to show everyone what a good and brave swimmer I am, I thought and ignored her warnings, continuing my stalking position for jumping into the lake. Diego got my message.

"We are not sure how deep this lake is and what kind of water it has; still, I request your permission to allow Benz to search at the bottom of the lake," he said to Gaspar.

"Why, in your opinion, this water has a such dark color, Armando?" asked Gaspar.

"I am not yet sure, but this dark color is probably due to turbulence created by mixing terrestrial river waters running to the sea under the coastal *'dientes de perro'* with the salty ocean waters brought by the tide," suggested Armando. "Changes in tides will cause the salty water to penetrate the river current inwards, creating turbulence and change of color on the surface."

"Sounds not dangerous; Benz got the scent. I believe we must allow him to follow it," suggested Diego.

"Not before my divers will get ready to accompany Benz," intervened Alejandro. "Nobody knows what kind of waters are in this lake, its color is dark, and the visibility appears to be very poor. We might need more lights to see the underwater bottom in such dark water," he ordered his divers to change into their surface water diving gear.

As soon as Diego released my leash, I jumped into the lake water and started paddling in its very cold water towards the center of the lake, where the scent of ore was stronger. The navy divers wearing scuba diving equipment went into the water as well. Suddenly, probably disturbed by our water jumps, the bats from the ceiling came down as missiles on the diver's heads in the water. I had to turn back to kill one of them and rip the wings of others before they could fly off.

This time, the divers followed me as I paddled to the center of the lake, but when I submerged, the incoming tide was so strong that I could barely swim against it. The strange blind white fish, which I have never before seen in my life, was moving around us, curious to see us. I learned to hold my breath while swimming and diving on our beach in Tarara before gulping the water. When diving on the beach of Tarara, I was told that I would be fine to hold my breath for about three minutes, which is even longer than untrained humans can. The navy divers followed me to the location of the scent. It was not easy, I never practiced deep diving intentionally, and I didn't know how deep I really could dive.

Down, down, I dived till my paws grew tired and hardly moved. After a while, the pressure on my eardrums started causing me pain, and there was a buzzing in my head. The air from my lungs went in a great explosive rush. The bubbles rubbed and bounded like tiny balloons against my nose and eyes as they took their upward flight.

It happened when the scent of golden ore became especially very strong. At that very moment, I saw a huge, nearly three times my length, massive golden cross lying on the bottom, surrounded by numerous boxes filled with different golden objects, barrels, and clay jars filled with gold, as well as baskets with golden bars. Colors and radiances pervaded me, I was losing my mind, there was no oxygen left in my lungs, and unless I allow myself to return to the surface, I will die; I knew that and allowed my body to float back to the surface. Diego jumped into the water immediately after noticing my head pocked up on the surface; he fetched and carried me to the lakeshore where Rubia, Pipo, and Paco were waiting.

Pipo and Paco got me out of the water and put me down to lie on the floor. Pipo pressed on my chest, and life returned to my lungs. Rubia licked my face, eyes, and my paws for a good half an hour until I completely recovered. She told me that I scared them, that I was a long time under the water, and they became afraid that I was dead.

I stood up to shake myself from head to tail, a dog shower of seawater raining down across my rescuers. Rubia decided to cheer me up. She took one stiff-legged leap to the left and one to the right, with her head down as if ready for play!

"Not to worry," I said, "I found their treasure. My job for humans is completed, and now we deserve to be left alone to enjoy our being together."

Meanwhile, Diego was helped to the lake's shore, and he came to pet me and checked me for injuries the best he knew. Paco and Pipo stood beside him, still worried about me.

"You must be careful with Benz," said Paco, "the longer than a few minutes diving will slow the heart rate and decrease blood and oxygen flow in the body of dogs. The excess liquid will collect in a dog's lungs and affect them in hours; keep a close eye on Benz."

I had plopped myself down at Diego's feet and licked his hand; then, I stood up beside Rubia, leaning on her with my body because my head was still going in rounds.

The rest of the humans were anxiously waiting for the return of divers with their report about what I had found and what they saw for themselves on the bottom of the lake. When divers finally surfaced and were helped to the sideline of the lake, they spoke with Alejandro in a low voice. After a while, Alejandro called Paco to join them. Gaspar, without a special invitation, rushed to join them as well. They probably discussed the report of divers and argued about something. We could not hear. Then the divers took the underwater video camera with more lights and went once again down the lake while Paco was writing and drawing something.

Thinking that my function was completed, I lay down with Rubia beside Diego and Pipo. We drank the fresh water, and I was offered a bite with meat, which I gave all to Rubia because I still felt dizzy and nauseous. Armando was looking with curiosity at Paco and the divers, who were devising some plans. We felt a bit resentful of them for not sharing with us their plans. When Paco joined us, he discussed with Armando the possibility that three hundred sixty years ago, the ocean tide was lower, and the treasures were deposited on a dry floor in a depressed area inside the cave, which became a subterranean lake today due to both processes of higher tide and erosion of karst cracks by the subterranean rivers.

On the divers' return, after they gave a new report, including a video, we were told not to discuss today's events with anyone, including our families, and to pack up our possessions for an immediate return to the camp. I was glad because I still didn't feel normal, my paws were wobbling when I attempted to walk, and I felt cold. Rubia suggested that I needed to rest under the sun to recover. When we exited, we got surprised by the red dusk and warmer temperatures. The time flew fast.

That evening we didn't hunt because I did not feel strong enough. Actually, I still felt weak and nauseous. Alejandro and Gaspar drove to the Roncali base, where they spoke to their bosses on the phone. On their return, Gaspar and Geovani feeling very happy and exhilarated, left for their hotel in Maria La Gorda. Gaspar told Diego that they would return tomorrow morning to pick us up for our return drive home. The rest of the pack ate dinner with yesterday's leftovers from the wild boar. Diego was also happy, but not Rubia and me. After dinner, we lay together by the campfire, and I proposed to her marriage. I explained to her that I was in love with her and wanted to live with her and our future pups.

To that end, I said, "I will ask my adoptive parents in Tarara to adopt you and our pups as well when they come. There is plenty of space in our large house, and I am sure that having fulfilled my task of finding the treasure for Comandante Tainted, I provided the safety and respect for our happy and peaceful existence."

"I am also very much in love with you," replied Rubia. "Still, I can't abandon Pipo - my human dad. He can't survive in a forest without his loyal girl-dog, he was always good to me, and I am not a traitor."

"Please try to change your mind," I begged. "If my parents adopt you, you and our pops will become, just like me, Cuban dogs with the rights of foreigners."

"No, my beloved Benz, sorry. I can't abandon Pipo. It will be wrong, and I am a loyal Cuban and will live and die as one. Patria o Muerte!"

"You are mistaken, my love," I said. "It is much better to be foreign in Cuba. Still, I love you so much that if you don't want to come with me to become adopted by my parents, I will explain our situation to them and will ask their permission to be adopted by Pipo to join you and him in your forester job."

"Don't be silly, Benz," she answered, "I don't live in a house. I am kept outside in a barn with other animals Pipo keeps. I am not saying it is a bad life, but we have a very strenuous hard job, and I am not certain at all that Pipo wants to take responsibility for a second dog and our future puppies because he is poor. Anyway, your short fur will not protect you from the clouds of mosquitos in the barn. You are used to the luxury life with the air conditioner."

"Please don't do it to me, my darling. I am ready to give up all my comforts as a Cuban who became a foreigner for life with you and our future puppies. As a forester, I am willing to walk with you side by side for the forty kilometers of coastal coastline. We must beg Pipo tomorrow, and if he concedes, I will ask my adoptive parents to bless our marriage," I concluded, and we licked each other noses in agreement.

Epilogue

I felt sad on our return to Tarara. My beautiful beloved Rubia, how I was missing her. The huge empty hole in my stomach and my heart hearts. No, I don't want any food. I was not even interested in observing what was happening outside of our car windows. Last night Diego and Pipo were marveling at both of us lying side by side, licking our snouts, and they discussed our amorous relationship. Diego told me that he asked his opinion of Pipo if Rubia and I could stay together with him, but Pipo was not interested in becoming an owner of an expensive Doberman. He worried that his job and living conditions were too hard and humble for an expensive breed of dog. His prime occupation was of the forester and not of the breeder. His family lived in a small peasant hut, and his wife and children were working on a state farm. They could not afford for their small place to be overrun by Doberman pups.

Diego himself was more worried about Mommy Dora and Daddy Frank becoming annoyed with him for allowing my romantic adventure. He was also afraid that they would disapprove of his recommendation to adopt Rubia and start a new family of mixed mongrels in Tarara.

Only a human mind can come up with such a paradox: our future puppies will be considered undesirable mongrels in Tarara, and Guanahacabibes as unadaptable Dobermans?

He tried to explain all this to us when Rubia and I attempted to glue ourselves to each other in the morning. It didn't help us. Rubia was forced to leave with Pipo and Juan back to the beach to help the turtles by cleaning the shore from sargasso, and I was dragged to take the seat with Diego in the car of Gaspar. Given my fulfilled mandate, Diego promised to talk to my adoptive parents about my amorous relationship with Rubia and ask them to deal with Pipo on my behalf.

We didn't stop at all on our way back, even to see red crabs, migrating in mass, like a red carpet, across the forest towards the beach. I continued to refuse the barbequed pieces of boar meat Diego brought with him for snacks during our travel; he started to worry about my health.

When we arrived that day at Tarara in the late afternoon, we were enthusiastically and lovingly met by Mommy Dora and Daddy Frank, who were overly happy to see us. They hugged and kissed me. Gogi jumped all over me and then suspiciously sniffed my body. He could smell the scent of Rubia all over me and immediately knew that I have sinned. He became very agitated and immediately wanted to hear my story.

I did not join Geovanni and Gaspar while they were talking to our parents in their office behind closed doors. For I was no longer interested in the treasure I found; all I could think was how badly I was missing Rubia. So, I stayed in the backyard with my adoptive brother Gogi to share with him my sadness about the separation from my beloved. Gogi understood my feelings because he, too, felt the same about Canelita.

In solidarity with me, he refused the food when Vera offered it to us and even attempted to feed us by hand. Only after Geovanni and Gaspar left did Gogi grant the favor to Vera and ate his food. I continued to abstain from food with the aim that Diego would have to explain to my adoptive parents the reason for my lack of appetite and sadness. I hoped that my abstinence would create substantial pressure on my parents, motivating them to seek my reunion with Rubia. When they asked if I was sick and why I was looking depressed and refused the food, Diego was forced to admit that I fall in love with Rubia and was missing her company. While being very happy and proud of our success in finding the treasure, Mommy and Daddy were also surprised with me and annoyed with Diego for my amorous condition.

"This ended your carrier Benz as a 'Holy Dog'" they said and promised to talk with Pipo about what could be done. All I could think was, *"When? How soon? And where my beautiful beloved and I could live together?"*

Eventually, after a couple of days, the pain of hunger made me accept my food, but I stopped sleeping on my parent's bed as a message to them that I would return there only after my beloved could join me on it. Until then, I was soaking in my loneliness under the desk in their bedroom, just to remind them how sad I was and how much I am missing my dear Rubia. Gogi used this opportunity to call me 'a cry-baby', but I don't care. My parents were also told about the strict secrecy requested by the Cuban military from everyone involved in the search for treasures at Cabo de San Antonio. "Remember, nobody is allowed to drop a word about the cave we found. Spreading any rumors about it will be considered treason," warned Alejandro.

Meanwhile, probably thanks to the protection of Comandante Tainted and my successful search for lost treasures, the status of our Joint Venture in Cuba and the relationship with our Cuban boss Colonel Beltran changed towards the temporal peaceful co-existence. We received the highest permission to continue working with our old Cuban personnel under the same conditions specified in our initial contract. Colonel Beltran stopped his aggressive visits to our office.

Neither Zoonosis for Dogs nor Zoonosis for Humans attacked our office in Tarara again, and we were allowed to walk on the beach and streets of Tarara without fear of persecution. Only my personal situation with Rubia continued to be sad. Diego, mommy, and daddy were trying to contact Pipo and Rubia but could not yet reach them because Pipo was temporarily transferred to an undisclosed location. My adoptive parents and Diego promised to tell me as soon as they have.

Then I learned of a new, very important development that shook all of Cuba. The return of the Vatican to Cuba! After the celebrations of the New Year, during which we were receiving the biggest number of visitors for delicious meals, the news of the forthcoming visit of Pope John Paul II to Cuba at the invitation of Fidel Castro himself made a huge splash.

A public campaign brought the island into a frenzy. All streets received a new makeup, all main roads were repaired, all walls were repainted, and huge religious posters with the image of the Pope were posted everywhere. According to some comments from our Cuban friends, Cuban institutions, schools, universities, and workplaces, all media were preparing the Cuban people to give the Vatican a loving welcome after the thirty-six years of religious persecution on the island.

When Gaspar came to chat in secret with my parents in Tarara, they all hugged me and laughed, commenting that the Cuban Catholic religion was revived thanks to Benz, the Gold-ore Superdog. Gaspar said that the treasures recovered from the cave are currently in the desalination laboratory, and they will be returned to their divine owner in exchange for badly needed foreign currency for Cuban purchases abroad, including food and medicine from the USA.

When Gaspar was delicately asked if there will be any personal benefits for the bosses - elite members of the Cuban government, he commented something about their new housing and '*boberias*' (the small items) in the form of television sets and video players, and some other items for entertainment according to their needs.

Hearing this, I thought to myself, *What a great example of human selfishness. I found for them the lost treasure of The Cathedral of Merida. I believe it permitted the Vatican to recover its property and reopen Catholicism in Cuba. Fidel Castro came to be recognized not only as a revolutionary but also as a benevolent and moral Catholic. Now he is sanctified from the paradise on Earth directly to the paradise in eternity. The Cuban people, once again, may pray for themselves and the Cuban government if they wish. The Cuban government was granted the hard currency for purchases abroad at a premium, including the entertainment equipment for elites.*

All I wanted was to be reunited with my beloved Rubia, but even after I risked my life for the treasures when diving deep inside the cave, the humans would not respect my only desire. I miss my beloved. There is no fairness, only a dog life in Cuba.

About the Author

Paulina Zelitsky is a Canadian Professional Engineer specializing in Ocean Engineering. Born in Odessa, Ukraine, Soviet Union, she started her career as a port designer for Soviet, Cuban, and later in the 70s for private Canadian engineering companies across Canada. After Paulina's naturalization and certification as a Canadian Professional Engineer, she jump-started her new career in the ocean and energy sectors. Paulina headed a Canadian Joint Venture in Cuba, mandated to survey the deep ocean waters of Guanahacabibes – the westernmost point of the Island of Cuba for seven years.

Other Amazon published books authored by Paulina:

The Sea is Only Knee Deep - volume 1,

The Sea is Only Knee Deep - volume 2,

Odessaphile: Jews in Odessa – a Story of Cultural Cross-Pollination/

Adios Angelina, English version

Adios Angelina, Spanish Version

Acknowledgments

I am grateful to my family and friends, especially my husband Paul and my children, for putting up with me while I was working on this book. My particular thanks go to Paul for early reading and Julie Tapanes, my editor and proofreader. For inspiration: Michael Bulgakov, Franz Kafka, Jack London, Damien Lewis, Asher Kravitz, Virginia Woolf, Curtis Moser, and Ralf Hardy.

Manufactured by Amazon.ca
Bolton, ON